MY FRIEND JENNI

MY FRIEND JENNI

Peter Rogers

Book Guild Publishing
Sussex, England

First published in Great Britain in 2005 by
The Book Guild Ltd
25 High Street
Lewes, East Sussex
BN7 2LU

Typesetting in Baskerville by
IML Typographers, Birkenhead, Merseyside

Printed in Great Britain by
CPI Bath

A catalogue record for this book is
available from The British Library

ISBN 1 85776 953 8

There was something different about Jon Stern. Mary, his mother, used to say that although she was aware of genes and that sort of thing, there was nothing in either of their families that could apply to him. He was a very good-looking boy, which was unusual in itself when applied to the family. He was neither clever nor athletic. He was almost backward at school. He did not appear to be interested in the opposite sex. He had no hobbies, unless music could be called a hobby, for he would spend hours tinkering on the piano in the front room. He was 'put to the piano', as the saying goes, at an early age by the local lady teacher, who happened to be the teacher at Grantley Grammar School when he went there.

There was nothing unusual, though, about the Stern family. They lived in a semi-detached house in a suburb north of London. Nor was the house itself unusual, though some unusual events were to take place there. It was the type of house that could be seen sprawling all over the country in rash ribbons. It had a garage to one side of it which acted as a buffer to one of the houses next door, the other side being actually built onto the other house. There was one bay window at ground level and one above, and a single window over the front door indicating a small bedroom. Inside the house a straight staircase rose to the well of the landing, off which were the bedrooms and the bathroom; one front, one back and a small one over the hall. All the houses in Maple Road were the same. In the front was a small garden giving access to the road, which was tree-lined. There was a larger garden at the rear, which itself backed onto the rear garden of the house in the next road.

Sam Stern, the owner of the house, was an accountant who commuted to the City each day where he worked for a large firm of finance consultants. He was a not unattractive man in his early forties but not particularly imaginative or enterprising, which probably accounted for the fact that he was not in business on his own.

Mary, his wife, was a few years his junior and had been a very popular girl in her youth. She was still attractive, having kept her figure. Her blonde hair, which was short, was natural. She was considered the more companionable of the two when it came to socialising. It was a question of attitude; whereas Sam was inclined to be introspective, Mary was gregarious. She would urge her husband forward where he would otherwise hesitate. Yet she was in no way domineering.

Their son, Jon, had inherited his mother's good looks and at fourteen years of age, attended the local school, which was within walking distance of his home. He was quiet, even morose. He never became interested in anything, except music. The girls in the school considered him dull and not worth bothering with. The boys avoided him. He went through school like an automaton, never excelling in any subject, except his precious music. He was like a bird waiting to be hatched.

The lives of the Stern family were uninteresting to anyone but themselves. Routine was the operative word; television and summer holidays by the sea being their only diversions. They had a small family car, which was used at week-ends or for holidays and was only changed when it became absolutely necessary. And it was at the time of the changing of the car that the routine of the Stern household became disturbed.

Jon was in his room upstairs, doing his homework. While he was puzzling over an essay he heard a female voice say:

'Can't you do it, Jon?'

Jon sat upright, startled. He looked about the room. He could not make out where the voice had come from.

He assumed he must have imagined it, because there was nobody else in the room.

'I'll help you if you like,' the voice said again.

At that Jon ran out of the room and downstairs to the sitting room, where his mother and father were watching television. He burst into the room, so agitated that Mary looked up in alarm.

'Jon,' she cried, 'what's the matter?'

'Is there someone in the house?' he asked, urgently.

'Only us, dear,' Mary assured him.

'I heard a voice.'

'Heard what?' asked Sam, suddenly interested.

'A woman's voice,' Jon explained. 'I heard it upstairs.'

'Too much computer gazing,' decided Sam, returning to the television screen.

'Come and sit down, Jon,' urged Mary, anxiously.

'No,' said Jon quietly. 'I'll go back.'

He went out of the room slowly, climbed the stairs to his own room, went in and shut the door. He looked about the room again but could see nothing out of the ordinary. He felt a bit shaky and cold, and a little frightened and wondered if he should ask his mother to arrange for him to see a doctor.

'No,' said the voice. 'You don't need to see a doctor. You're quite sane.'

'Good Lord,' exclaimed Jon. 'You knew what I was thinking.'

'Yes, Jon. I'm a spirit.'

'A ghost, you mean?'

'No. I'm not a ghost.'

'But you're dead?'

'Oh, I know that's what you call it. But nobody dies, Jon. The spirit leaves the body and lives on. Like me.'

'You're not an alien or anything, are you?'

'No. My name is Jenni.'

3

Jon was feeling calmer now. More relaxed.

'Oh. Hello, Jenni.'

'Hello, Jon.'

'How do you know me? I mean, why pick on me?'

'Every now and then we decide to help someone and I decided to help you.'

'Why?'

'Because I thought you needed it.'

'I certainly do,' agreed Jon with a laugh.

'You could call me your Guardian Angel.'

Jon moved away from the door and slumped in his chair.

'I'm going mad. I know it.'

'No, you're not, Jon. I told you that. Try to accept me.'

'How? How can I? I can't see you.'

'No. I'm afraid you can't see me. But from now on I'll be beside you all the time.'

'Where are you now?'

'Sitting on your bed.'

'Oh.'

'It's alright. I won't upset it. I don't take up any room and I don't leave any dents.'

'That's good. It could be awkward otherwise. Especially at school.'

'When I talk to you, Jon, no-one can hear but you.'

'If I go about talking to you, people will think I really am mad.'

'You don't need to speak out. You can talk to me in your mind.'

'What? How?'

'You've done it before. You've had imaginary conversations, haven't you?'

'Oh. Yes.'

'That's all you have to do.'

'What do you look like, Jenni?'

'Oh, that's hard to say. I don't really have features. Physical features.'

'You must have had at some time.'

'I seem to remember black hair, short with a fringe. Like a boy.'

'I have a cousin who looks like that. Pam. I like her.'

'I know you do.'

'I don't see her very often. She lives in London. She's my age. How old are you, Jenni?'

'There's no such thing as age with us.'

'That's handy.'

'It is, isn't it?' agreed Jenni, with a laugh.

'I'm fourteen.'

'I know.'

There was a silence, during which Jon looked about the room.

'Are you looking for me?' asked Jenni.

'Yes. You're not on the bed now, are you?'

'No. I'm by the table. It's clever of you to notice.'

'I felt it. The sound moved.'

'Good. That means you've accepted me.'

'Does it?'

'I'm glad.'

'Will I only be able to talk to you here?'

'Out loud, yes. It depends who's about. I'll always be behind you, following you about, so don't worry.'

'I must say I like talking to you. It's company.'

'It is for me, too.'

'Yes. I suppose it could be lonely up there.'

'It is at times.'

'Could I talk to you out loud downstairs in front of the family if I explained to them?'

'Oh, yes. But you won't find that easy.'

'I can try.'

'You haven't finished your homework yet.'

5

'Oh, it's only an essay. I can manage that.'

'You looked puzzled just now.'

'Well, it's called "On getting up in the morning" and I was wondering how to go about it.'

'What have you decided?'

'I was thinking of saying how difficult it was as a schoolboy when you have to get up to go to school. It's not as if you're on your hols and you can go cycling. Then you get up eagerly. Then, of course, there are the seasons. It's different getting up in the summer and winter. Then I could put in the bit about lying in on Sundays.'

'Don't you like getting up in the morning?'

'Not when I have to go to school.'

'You'll like school more when you do better at your lessons.'

'How am I going to do that?'

'With my help.'

'The only period I like at school is music. With Miss Molloy.'

'She's very good.'

'Funny old lady. I think–'

Jenni interrupted the boy, who was inclined to talk.

'Don't you think you should get on with your essay?'

'Yes. Might as well, I suppose.'

Jon proceeded to write in his exercise book. As he wrote he was carried away, as usual, by his subject. He enjoyed writing essays and forgot about Jenni while he composed his sentences, unaware of her promised omnipresence.

He did not say anything about Jenni when he said goodnight to his mother and father. That night he enjoyed a dreamless sleep and did not think of Jenni again until he was dressing and getting ready to go downstairs to breakfast.

'Are you there, Jenni?', he asked quietly.

6

'Yes. I'm here,' she replied from somewhere in the room.

'I'm going down to breakfast.'

'I'll be with you.'

Sam and Mary were already seated at the breakfast table when Jon came into the room. His breakfast was set out for him.

'Morning,' said Jon, cheerfully.

'Good morning,' said Sam and Mary together.

'Ah!' breathed Jon as he sat down.

'You're very happy this morning, dear,' suggested Mary, 'considering it's school.'

'Am I?' Then, suddenly: 'We need another chair.'

'What for?' asked Mary.

'Oh, no,' Jon corrected himself. 'You don't take up any room, do you?'

'What are you on about?' demanded Sam.

'I was talking to Jenni,' Jon explained.

'Who?' asked Mary, in alarm.

'Jenni,' repeated Jon.

'Who's Jenni?' asked Sam.

'A friend of mine.'

'Oh?' said Mary, noncommitally.

'When I came downstairs last night,' Jon went on, 'I said I heard a female voice.'

'Yes?' prompted Mary.

'It was Jenni,' said Jon.

Neither Sam nor Mary said any more. They exchanged worried glances. By mutual body language they decided not to pursue the subject. To avoid a discussion about something he didn't understand, Sam interrupted.

'The new car's being delivered this evening.'

'Oh,' exclaimed Jon, successfully diverted, 'I'll miss the old banger.'

'So will I,' put in Mary, with some relief.

The make of car, chosen after long discussions and the perusal of countless brochures, was the latest Sabu, a Japanese vehicle, with all the extras and gadgets included in the price. They had all ridden in the demonstration car and expressed approval.

Jon left for school that morning with no further mention of Jenni, much to the relief of his parents. As soon as the front door closed Mary turned to her husband.

'What do you make of that?' she asked.

'Someone he dreamed about, I expect,' replied Sam.

'I thought he'd gone funny.'

'Funny?'

'Yes. Doesn't it worry you?'

'No. Kids have little fantasies.'

'Kids? He's fourteen.'

'That's nothing to go by.'

'He wanted somewhere for her to sit. That's not fantasy. What did he say her name was?'

'Jenni.'

'I wonder where that name comes from.'

'I shouldn't think the name means anything.'

'I hope not.'

'Don't worry, dear. I tell you, it's fantasy.'

'If it was a dream,' persisted Mary, 'you'd think he'd have forgotten by the time he came down to breakfast.'

'Perhaps it was a dream about someone nice. He was certainly more cheerful than usual.'

'Someone he fell in love with, you mean?'

'Something like that.'

'In that case I think he'd be more likely to keep it to himself.'

'He obviously let the name slip out.'

'What about that bit about you don't take up much room? That could be a ghost.'

'Don't be silly. There are no such things. When you're his age you fall in and out of love all the time. I remember at Christmas time I used to fall in love with the Principal Boy in pantomime.'

'That's always a girl.'

'Exactly. It's a wonder pantomime doesn't turn all kids gay.'

'You and your pantomime. Panto and Peter Pan. That's your answer to everything.'

Sam looked at the clock on the kitchen wall.

'I must be off,' he announced.

Mary saw her husband off to the office with the peremptory peck on the cheek and a wave from the front door. He then began his walk to the station.

Mary's first task once she had said goodbye to her husband and shut the front door was to clear away the breakfast things and wash up. While she was doing that she thought about her son's behaviour. She was not prepared to dismiss the incident as easily as her husband seemed to be able to do. If the boy had had a beautiful dream and fallen in love with a girl called Jenni, it was unlikely that be would want to broadcast the fact to all and sundry, least of all to his parents. He was a strange boy, sensitive and caring, but not all that bright scholastically. She was aware of that. His school reports had always been disappointing, especially to her husband, whose accountant's mind was offended particularly by the boy's failure in mathematics. Why did Jon ask where Jenni was going to sit? Did she walk down the stairs with him? Was she in the bathroom with him? Such practical questions needed answering. Then he'd said 'Oh, you don't take up any space, do you?' That all suggested some kind of apparition, she decided.

Mary remembered an odd occasion when Jon was ten years old. He'd made his way upstairs to bed, then he came down again and said that he'd seen Granny on the landing. Granny at that time was ill in hospital. Sam had laughed and said 'Don't be silly,' and went upstairs with the boy to show him that there was nobody there. As Sam returned to the hall, the telephone rang. It was the hospital, announcing that Granny had just died. At the time it made Mary wonder if Jon really had seen Granny on the landing. Could it be that Jon was slightly psychic and Jenni was some visitation from the past? In that case, what did her appearance mean and who was she? She couldn't remember anyone named Jenni either on her side of the family or Sam's. She wanted to ask someone if they'd ever heard Jon mention the name of Jenni. But who could she ask? Jon hadn't made any friends at school that she knew of. Or was she worrying too much, as Sam suggested?

After a certain amount of perfunctory dusting and cleaning Mary set out for the shops. She walked to the nearest bus stop, which was at the end of the road, carrying a raffia shopping basket. She had to wait for the bus and while she stood there she couldn't help thinking again of Jon and this Jenni person. It seemed that the problem would never leave her. As she saw the bus coming she fiddled in her purse to find the exact fare, a chore which she found tedious. She wished for the return of the days when conductors were engaged to take fares and give you change. Another man on the bus would also be protection for the driver, she thought. She was travelling to the local supermarket but she wasn't intending to buy very much because she wouldn't be able to carry it on the bus. Once a month when she had a larger order she was allowed to take the car. She was a very good driver and critical of her husband's driving.

On arriving back home she cooked herself a snack for lunch, a Welsh rarebit. It was all she wanted and she sat at the kitchen table to eat it alone. The afternoon would be devoted to ironing and sewing and after that she would make herself a cup of tea and set out the cakes and so on for Jon's return from school. By then she would have tidied herself up, changing from the outfit designated 'mornings', to something less utilitarian. She was always pleased when either Jon or Sam came home. She felt lonely during the day with no-one to talk to and tried to ward off the loneliness by keeping herself busy. Sam, of course, had his colleagues at the office for company.

Jon always appeared to be hungry at teatime. He would enjoy the chocolate layered cake and the fish paste on bread and butter. She wondered if he would mention Jenni again.

Actually, he made a surprising remark when he did sit down to tea.

'I enjoyed school today,' he said brightly.

'That makes a change,' commented Mary.

She knew that Jon normally hated school, probably because he never did very well with his lessons.

While he was busy eating he said, 'Jenni helped me.'

Mary felt a sinking feeling in her stomach and she was too taken aback to make a sensible remark, so she simply asked, 'Is she one of the teachers?'

'No, silly!' protested Jon. 'My friend.'

Echoes of breakfast time, thought Mary. She wished that her husband was with her. She didn't think she could cope with the conversation on her own.

'Oh, that's nice,' was all she could think to say.

She studied her son closely. He didn't seem to be any different, a little happier if anything. Yet something must have happened to him to bring about this odd obsession.

11

'Have you got a headache?' she asked.

'Headache? No. Why?'

'Where did you meet this Jenni?'

'I haven't actually met her. Not face to face. I told you, she came upstairs last night. I can't see her. I can only hear her.'

'You said she helped you at school.'

'Yes.'

'How?'

'She talks to me.'

'Tells you the answers, you mean?'

'Not only that. She explains things to me. You can get answers out of a crib but that wouldn't tell you how to do it.'

'I see.'

She didn't 'see' at all. She was at a complete loss. 'Does anybody else know about Jenni?' she asked.

'No. I only told you.'

'No. What I mean is, does Jenni talk to other people apart from you?'

'I don't think so. I don't know why she picked on me.'

'Didn't you ask her?'

'I did. In a way.'

'What was her answer?'

'She said she thought I needed help.'

'A lot of people need help. What does she sound like? Young or old?'

'Like you.'

'Where does she come from? Outer space?'

'Oh, no. I made sure of that. I don't want anything to do with that. She just turned up. She said she was a spirit.'

'What a pity we can't see her.'

'She says she has black hair and a fringe. Like Pam.'

'Where is she now?'

'Somewhere around.'

'But where?'

'I don't know. I'll ask her if you like?'

'Ask her then.'

'Where are you, Jenni?'

'Right beside you, Jon.'

'She says she's right beside me.'

Involuntarily, Mary moved away as if in somebody's way. 'I didn't hear anything,' she complained. 'I didn't hear anything, Jenni,' Mary added.

'You can't speak to her. It's just me and Jenni.'

'I don't think that's right. She shouldn't influence you against me.'

'She's not doing that. She's helping me. You should be pleased.'

'Well, I'm not happy about it. Neither is your father.'

Jon got up from the table suddenly. 'You don't understand. I'm going upstairs,' he declared.

This was the usual routine after tea, so Mary was not alarmed. He would stay up there until there was something he wanted to see on television. As she pondered over Jon's remarks, she poured herself another cup of tea. She hoped that she could remember what he had said, so as to be able to repeat it to her husband. She was really worried now because it was obvious that this Jenni person was not as fanciful as she had hoped. Sam's idea of it being a beautiful dream had no substance.

When Jon shut the door of his room he called out, 'You there, Jenni?'

'Yes. I'm here, Jon.'

'I wish I could see you.'

'That wouldn't be a very good idea.'

'Why not?'

'You'd keep looking at me when I said something and that would be embarrassing for you and for me. At

13

present you don't react when I say something. You didn't at school today. You don't want people to think you have someone sitting on your shoulder like a parrot.'

'You're probably right. It's a shame, though.' Suddenly Jon had an idea. 'If you were a ghost,' he exclaimed, 'I could see you.'

'A ghost only haunts one spot,' explained Jenni. 'I can go anywhere.'

'That's true. I wouldn't like it if you were only in this room.'

Mary was unaware of her son's discussion with Jenni. She cleared away the tea things. She couldn't begin to prepare the evening meal as she had no idea when the car was being delivered.

At six-thirty Sam arrived home. It was always the same time. His first thought, once he had settled down, was the whereabouts of Jon.

'Where's the boy?' he asked.

'Upstairs in his room,' replied Mary.

'On the internet, I suppose.'

'I always think that's dangerous.'

'Why?'

'Don't some girls meet up with people on the internet and vanish?'

'I can't imagine anyone wanting to kidnap Jon.'

'Perhaps he'd like to kidnap someone himself.'

'Why? Has he mentioned that girl again?'

'Jenni? Yes. He had quite a lot to say about her at tea. I wish I could remember it all.'

'What can you remember?'

'He said he enjoyed school today.'

'That's unusual.'

'He said it was because Jenni helped him.'

'What!'

'He was quite pleased with himself.'

'Perhaps he'll have a better report this term.'

'I wouldn't bank on it.'

'Why? Don't you think it'll last?'

'I don't see how it can and I'm not sure I want it to, school report or not.'

'I was only kidding about that.'

'Who is Jenni? Where does she come from? I asked him. He doesn't know. She's some kind of spirit, he says.'

'Oh, God! Don't tell me we're into that kind of rubbish. Table tapping and all that.'

'I wouldn't call it rubbish.'

'I haven't patience with it.'

'According to Jon, this person is quite genuine.'

'Oh, I'm sure. How can she be, for God's sake?'

Sam had become quite indignant and agitated.

'You'd better talk to Jon about it, not me,' Mary complained.

'I will. If he's got some crack-brained idea in his head…'

'I suggest you keep your patience in case he goes back into his shell, then we'll never know what's happening.'

'You sound as if he's convinced you.'

'No. But it's not what we thought at breakfast. It's more real than that.'

'Real? Does he know what she looks like?'

'Black hair with a fringe like Pam's.'

'He's seen her?'

'No. She told him.'

'He's been looking at those space things on television. They have black hair with a fringe. That's what it's all about.'

'That wouldn't help him at school, would it?'

'I don't know how he was helped at school.'

'You'll have to ask him.'

'Didn't you?'

'No.'

'Why not?'

'It's no good putting it all on me,' accused Mary, petulantly.

'I always thought mothers were closer than fathers to their children.'

'A good way out.'

Their little quarrel, gentle as it was, was interrupted by Jon joining them.

'What time's the car arriving, Dad?' he asked.

'The man said seven o'clock. I'd better get ours out.'

'I'll come with you,' said Jon. 'I'd like to say goodbye to old Tinker Bell.'

He followed his father out to the garage.

'Better take everything out,' Mary called out to them.

Sam drove the car out of the garage and left it in the front of the house. He got out of it, gave it a pat on the roof in farewell and returned to the house. Jon lingered, walking round the car as if inspecting it. Sam and Mary watched him from the front window. They could see that he was talking to himself.

'I wonder what he's saying,' mused Mary.

'Some people get attached to their car,' explained Sam. 'They reckon they have a personality.'

When Jon came back to the house he declared, 'Jenni says she doesn't envy anyone driving in that.'

'How rude!' exclaimed Mary.

'There's nothing wrong with it,' protested Sam. 'It's stood us in good stead.'

'She says it's running into its troublesome period.'

'Well, of course it is,' agreed Sam. 'That's why we're changing it.'

'It stands to reason,' put in Mary.

Jon did not react to their criticism, he simply picked up his favourite magazine, flopped onto a chair and started to read.

At a few minutes past seven there was a ring on the front door bell.

'It's here!' cried Mary.

Jon put his book down and went to the window while Sam went to the front door.

'Here we are, Mr Stern,' said the car salesman, dangling the keys in front of him.

'Better take me over it again,' suggested Sam, 'in case I've forgotten something.'

The salesman led the way to the car and Sam followed. Mary and Jon were close behind them. Jon stood admiring the new shiny vehicle while Sam was re-introduced to the various buttons and gadgets.

'You like it, Jon?' asked Mary.

'Yes. I like dark blue.'

He then went on muttering to himself.

'Dad didn't want a pale colour. He likes dark blue. So do I.'

'What?' asked Mary, puzzled.

'Jenni was saying she prefers a light colour because it doesn't show the dirt.'

Mary had forgotten about Jenni in the excitement of the arrival of the car. She had forgotten that she and her husband had been discussing her at length but a short time ago.

'She may be right,' said Mary dismissively, not wishing to continue the conversation.

As soon as Sam's brief instruction was completed the salesman drove the old car away, watched almost tearfully by the family. As they stood on the pavement Mary suddenly suggested, 'It's such a lovely evening. Why don't we go for a drive?'

'Where to?' asked Sam, without enthusiasm.

'Anywhere,' Mary went on. 'Just a trip out into the country. It needn't be for long. We can eat when we get back. What do you say?'

'Alright,' agreed Sam. 'Coming, Jon?'

'Yes, I'll come.'

They all climbed into the car. Mary sat in the front seat next to Sam, and Jon clambered into the back seat, where he bounced up and down to test the upholstery. He looked around and found ash trays, window buttons and pockets for maps.

'Right,' said Sam. 'Off we go.'

They drove away beyond the built-up area to where there were open spaces with woods and farms acting as a kind of pastoral sandwich between sprawling dormitory towns.

'It's very comfortable in the back,' announced Jon.

'Good,' said Sam.

'Well, it is for me,' Jon went on. 'I don't know what kind of car you're used to.'

Sam and Mary exchanged significant glances. It was obvious that Jon was talking to Jenni.

'Oh, it's nice to get away from the house,' exclaimed Mary. 'Why don't we do this more often?'

'Because we all get too tired and lazy,' explained Jon. 'We wouldn't be doing this now if we didn't have a new car.'

'There is that,' admitted Mary.

'Mum would be too busy cooking dinner,' put in Jon.

'You're quite right,' agreed Mary. 'You see?' she went on, addressing her husband, 'someone appreciates what I do.'

Their brief evening tour took them through winding lanes, some of them with passing bays, causing Mary to cry out, 'Don't get it scratched!'

'I think we'd better turn back,' said Sam, fearfully.
'I've no idea where we are.'

'Jenni says the main road is left and left again,' urged
Jon.

'Oh, thanks,' said Sam. Once on the main road with
its rush of traffic,they found their way home quite easily.
As soon as they were home and indoors Mary said, 'I'll
get us something to eat.'

Sam went directly to the television set and pressed the
remote control button from station to station. Jon was
on his way upstairs when Mary called out, 'You staying
up there?'

'I've got my homework. I'll come down when you're
ready.'

When the boy was out of earshot Mary joined her
husband.

'You noticed that Jenni is still with us?' she remarked.

'I noticed. Yes.'

'What are we going to do?'

'Nothing. Let it fade out.'

'You think it will?'

'Bound to.'

'I hope you're right.'

'Don't worry about it, it's just a phase.'

Sam wouldn't have said it was just a phase if he had seen
his son tackling his homework. The subject was maths,
which he hated.

'You don't like maths, do you, Jon?' said Jenni.

'No. Hate it.

'Let's have a look.'

Jon spread his books out onto the table.

'Sit down and I'll tell you what to put,' commanded
Jenni.

19

Jon picked up his pen and prepared to write out Jenni's dictation. He put down figures without knowing what they meant. It was the sort of long equation that Mr Tripp, the maths master at school, would chalk up on the blackboard as an example. Jenni explained what the figures meant as they went along and Jon actually understood. Once he was shown the way, he was able to follow her and even enjoyed working out the equation with her.

When it was completed Jenni said, 'There, that wasn't so bad, was it?'

'No. I enjoyed that.'

'Good.'

'I just couldn't get started.'

'That's because you didn't want to.'

'Is it?'

Jon held up the book, admiring his work.

'Take that, old Tripp,' he exclaimed as he and Jenni laughed together.

When he came down to the meal that Mary had prepared he was quite cheerful. Usually when he had maths for his homework he was depressed all the evening.

'You're very pleased with yourself,' commented Mary. 'It's maths tonight, isn't it?'

'Yes. I'd like to see old Tripp's face tomorrow.'

'Why?'

'I think I've cracked it.'

'Do you want me to look at it?' asked Sam.

'No. That's not allowed.'

'Who's to know?'

'Me, for one.'

'Don't encourage him, dear,' advised Mary. 'You know the rules as well as he does.'

* * *

20

As a result of his homework, however, Jon had had to suffer extreme embarrassment at school next morning. It was during the maths lesson, of course; something that Jon usually abhorred because he couldn't understand what was going on. In spite of the fact that his father was an accountant, or because of it, he hated anything to do with figures. Words, yes. Or music. He was happy with those.

All the pupils in Jon's class were sitting quietly and obediently while Mr Tripp, the kindly, tweedy, middle-aged maths master, went through their homework on his desk. The pattern was familiar. The Lacey boy would be top and Jon would be bottom. On this occasion, though, the pattern was changed.

'That's odd,' mused Mr Tripp as he perused the exercise books. He had come to the end of the pile.

'Hand out the books, Lacey,' he commanded.

The sycophantic Lacey, a boy of Jon's age but with very short cropped fair hair and pale face, sprang out of his seat and ran up to Mr Tripp's desk. He gathered up the pile of exercise books in his arms and walked round the room handing them out. Everyone's name was on the front of their book. When he had returned to his seat Mr Tripp called out:

'Stern!'

'Sir,' said Jon obediently, standing up at his single desk.

'Did you have any help with your homework?'

'No, sir.'

'You're sure?

'Yes, sir.'

'Very odd,' muttered Mr Tripp.

Jon was still standing by his desk.

'Have I got it wrong, sir?'

'Wrong?' echoed Mr Tripp. 'No, Stern, you've got it right. That's what I don't understand.'

21

The rest of the class chuckled dutifully at their master's joke.

'You're usually near the bottom when it comes to maths and Lacey's at the top. But this time you're top and Lacey is only second.'

There was a muttering in the class, while Lacey looked hurt and angry.

'How do you account for that, Stern?' asked Mr Tripp.

'I don't know, sir,' replied Jon, feeling uncomfortable and wondering what was coming next.

'And you say you didn't have any help from your father?' Mr Tripp persisted.

'No, sir.'

'Have you suddenly woken up, do you think?'

Again the class tittered.

'I don't know, sir,' repeated Jon.

'Very well,' concluded Mr Tripp, 'I suggest we conduct a little experiment.'

Jon sat down. Mr Tripp gathered his black gown about him and made his way to the large blackboard attached to the wall of the room. He picked up a piece of chalk and began to write out a mathematical problem on the board. It was a difficult and complex problem but in keeping with the work represented in the homework in question. At the end of the problem Mr Tripp stood back and admired his own work.

'There you are, Stern,' he declared. 'Come and solve that. Here's the chalk.'

He held out the piece of chalk to Jon, who made no move to accept it.

'No, thank you, sir,' he said.

'What? You refuse?'

'I refuse to take part because it is suggesting that I am a liar.'

'How do you make that out?'

'You want to test me to prove I did my homework without help because you don't believe me.'

'Or is it because you can't do it?'

'I will do it if you withdraw your accusation.'

'Oh, I say. Hoity-toity.'

'I am not a liar, sir.'

The rest of the class looked on in fear and astonishment as Jon clashed with his master.

'Very well, Stern. I withdraw any suggestion or inference that you had help with your homework and invite you to show me and the class how you would tackle the equation you see on the blackboard.'

'Thank you, sir.'

The rest of the class breathed a sigh of relief as Jon, blushing and frightened, moved away from his desk and approached the blackboard, chalk in hand.

'Don't worry, Jon,' said Jenni. 'I'm with you.'

Only Jon could hear what she said, though it could be seen that he was muttering something to himself as if in answer to some request. As the equation was set out in rather a long line, he walked up and down studying it.

Mr Tripp, who had returned to his own desk, said, 'Take your time.'

All was quiet and tense as Jon began slowly to write figures on the board. Mr Tripp was the only one who could hear him making strange noises to himself as he progressed with the problem. And so it went on until, with Jenni's help, he came to the end of his task. With a flourish he drew a long line of chalk at the bottom of the blackboard.

'That's it, sir,' he said.

'And correct, too,' conceded Mr Tripp.

Jon returned to his desk and suddenly the rest of the class, with the exception of Lacey, burst into spontaneous applause. Mr Tripp allowed their enthusiasm to last a few seconds before silencing them.

'And why couldn't you have done that before?' he asked. 'Have you been asleep all this time?'

'Must have, sir,' admitted Jon, with a grin.

'You'll have to look to your laurels, Lacey,' warned Mr Tripp.

Lacey smirked complacently. Jon was perspiring profusely as he sat at his desk. He took out his handkerchief and mopped his face and forehead. He was relieved that the ordeal was over, an ordeal he could not have endured without the aid of Jenni, who had been prompting him all the time.

Fortunately for Jon, he was not obliged to undergo any further feats during the day and he made no outstanding contribution to the rest of the day's studies. The only event that concerned him was his confrontation with Lacey at the end of the day. Lacey, the school bully, tackled Jon as he was making for the gate on his way home.

'Who do you think you are, Stern?' challenged Lacey, putting his hand on the gate to prevent Jon from leaving.

'I beg your pardon?' asked Jon calmly.

'That was a lot of showing off, wasn't it?'

'I only did what Tripp asked me to do.'

'Well, don't go getting ideas.'

'Are you threatening me?'

'I'm warning you.'

'Don't start anything you might be sorry for, Lacey.'

Lacey was joined by his friend Harvey, another bully.

'What's going on?' Harvey asked.

'I'm just warning him,' said Lacey.

'Quite right,' agreed Harvey.

'And I'm warning both of you,' said Jon menacingly. 'Don't start anything.'

'Hark at him!' guffawed Harvey.

Jon unexpectedly grabbed hold of the lapels of Harvey's jacket with one hand and pulled him roughly to him. It was so uncharacteristic and surprising that both Harvey and Lacey were suddenly cowed.

'You heard me,' snorted Jon, pushing Harvey away from him.

He opened the gate without further hindrance and made his way home.

'Why didn't you hit him?' asked Lacy belligerently.

'Why didn't you?' countered Harvey.

Actually Jon had shown an aspect of his character that no-one had seen before and it frightened the two boys. Bullies that they were, they were not keen to engage in confrontation if there was the possibility of opposition.

Jon walked home alone, occupied with his own thoughts and talking to himself, which meant that he was talking to Jenni.

'No,' he was saying. 'I've never had a fight at school. They're a couple of bullies those two. They just annoyed me.'

After a few more steps he said, 'I didn't like doing that sum on the board. I had to do it because you'd helped me with my homework and old Tripp was suspicious. I solved it, with your help. But I didn't like doing it. I was sweating. I felt a fool out there on my own.'

Jon wondered how much he should tell his mother and father about the events of the day. How could he explain about Jenni helping him? They wouldn't understand. And would it be fair to Jenni to tell them? They knew about her, of course, but did they believe in her? He didn't know what to tell them and his anxiety showed in his demeanour when he arrived home – to such an extent that Mary feared that he had got into trouble at school.

Nothing was said during tea time apart from the usual platitudes, and it wasn't long before Jon made his way upstairs. Mary was concerned. Something had gone wrong, she felt sure. But what? She didn't like to ask. He would tell her in his own time, she hoped.

It wasn't until they were all sitting down to the evening meal that Mary decided to ask, 'Are you alright, Jon?',

'Yes.'

'You seem quiet.'

'I'm alright.'

'Everything alright at school?' asked Sam, anticipating the cause of the trouble.

Jon didn't answer at first. Then he said, 'Old Tripp asked me if you'd helped me with my homework.'

'Why?'

'Because I got it right.'

'He thought that was unusual, did he?'

'Yes.'

'Not very discriminating for a school master.'

'What did you say?' asked Mary.

'I said no.'

'Didn't he believe you?' Mary went on.

'I don't think so,' admitted Jon.

'Perhaps I should write to him,' suggested Sam.

'He made me solve a problem on the blackboard in front of the whole class,' complained Jon.

'Oh, did he?' exclaimed Sam, offended. 'Testing you, in other words. Cunning. How did you do?'

'It was very difficult. If I hadn't solved it he would have said you helped me.'

26

'Accused you of lying?'

'Yes.'

'Did you solve it?' asked Mary.

'Yes.'

'Good for you,' enthused Sam. 'We'll make an accountant of you yet.'

'No, thanks. Jenni helped me.'

'Who?' asked Sam, in surprise.

Then he hesitated. He'd forgotten about the Jenni person, the fictitious, invisible friend. He looked across at Mary, who looked frightened.

'How did she do that?' asked Sam, tentatively.

'She took me through it. Like she did last night.'

'So it was Jenni who helped you. You couldn't tell old Tripp that.'

'Hardly.'

'I wonder what he would have said,' mused Mary.

'He would have fallen through the floor,' suggested Jon, with a laugh.

'How real is this Jenni person, then?' asked Sam.

'Real enough to solve old Tripp's problem. I couldn't have done it alone,' said Jon.

'You can't see her?'

'No, Dad. She talks to me.'

'Why doesn't she talk to us?' asked Mary.

'She says she's a spirit sent only to help me.'

'Spirit?' scoffed Sam. 'What a lot of rot.'

'You don't understand,' complained Jon.

'I certainly don't. Why should she be sent to help you?'

'I don't know.'

'And who sent her?'

'I don't know that, either.'

'A not particularly bright schoolboy. I can't think why any spirit should take the trouble.'

'If it helps the boy,' suggested Mary.

'For how long?' continued Sam.

'Do you think it's anything to do with outer space?' ventured Mary.

'Heaven forbid!' cried Sam. 'We'd have every newspaper on our doorstep. Plus television.'

'I haven't told anybody,' Jon assured them. 'Only you.'

'We'd better be careful,' warned Sam. 'Especially with neighbours.'

'Don't worry,' soothed Mary.

'What does it all mean, Mother?' asked Jon anxiously.

'It means, dear,' replied Mary, 'that you have a guardian angel looking after you. You're very lucky. You should be grateful.'

'I don't feel lucky. I don't feel anything.'

'You never have,' said Sam. 'You just go about as if nothing matters.'

'You feel more confident, don't you, dear?' asked Mary. 'About your lessons?'

'Oh, yes. It's like having a crib.'

'You said that was cheating,' Sam reminded him. 'And another thing. Have you ever wondered how long this can go on?'

'You mean Jenni might go away?' asked Mary eagerly.

'She came all of a sudden,' explained Jon, 'so I suppose she can go all of a sudden. And then old Tripp will say it was a flash in the pan and I'll be back where I started.'

'At the bottom of the form,' asserted Sam.

'Yes.'

'You will have learned something, though, to tide you over,' put in Mary.

'Perhaps. I'm not very good at remembering things.'

'Jon,' began Mary again, 'did you see something on television to set this off?'

'How do you mean?'

'Well, there are programmes about things from outer space and that sort of thing.'

'I never watch those. I think they're silly.'

Sam made a significant gesture to Mary.

'We'll have to get used to this Jenni,' conceded Sam.

'Treat her like a daughter,' suggested Mary.

'I must get back to my homework,' declared Jon.

Once Jon was out of the room Mary put her finger to her lips to warn her husband not to say anything. She went to the door to make sure that Jon was out of earshot. When she returned to her armchair she said, 'Well?'

'I thought it best to humour him.'

'So did I. But treating her like a daughter and all that, Heaven forbid.'

'I wonder if he shouldn't see a doctor,' suggested Sam.

'Whatever for? He's not sick.'

'A psychiatrist.'

'He's not mad, either.

'I don't like it, though.'

'Go with it, dear,' Mary advised. 'It's not hurting him or us.'

'What if it gets worse?'

'How worse?'

'It could become an obsession. Send him over the top.'

'He seems to be in control at the moment.'

'All the same, I think I'll have a word with Doctor Hall,' decided Sam.

'What will you tell him?'

'I'll tell him what we know.'

'I wouldn't want him questioning Jon.'

'Why not?'

'Because it would frighten him. It would be going back on our word,' argued Mary.

29

'What word?'

'You said we'd have to get used to her and I said treat her like a daughter. We can't suddenly have her exorcised or whatever they call it.'

'It won't hurt if I have a word with Doctor Hall.'

'And let him think your son's not right in the head? Charming.'

'Oh, well. We'll see.'

On such a note of near antagonism Mary and Sam settled to watch television. In the morning no mention was made of Jenni. Jon sat down to his breakfast with hardly a word beyond a greeting. He automatically made room for Jenni as he sat down and then corrected himself, remembering that she did not take up any room. It had been a courtesy movement. Sam noticed the gesture and was about to comment:

'I thought...' he began.

Mary nudged him into silence. He wanted to ask why Jon should make room for Jenni when she was invisible. At length, Sam left for the office and Jon left for school. Mary was on her own, and all the time that she was busying herself about the house she was worrying about Jon and Jenni. She wondered if she could make contact with Jenni herself. After all, as the boy's mother she had a special interest. She would only try it in the house alone with nobody watching.

She stood in the middle of the room and called out, quietly, 'Jenni. Are you there?'

There was no reply, so she tried again.

'Jenni?'

Again there was no reply, so she gave up trying, feeling a little foolish at the same time. Jenni, she remembered, must be at school helping Jon with his lessons. The memory comforted her. For the hundredth time she wondered why this Jenni should pick on Jon.

He wasn't destined for anything out of the ordinary. He was just a normal boy. He would leave school, get a job, get married and have a family. Why bother to guide him at all? Why guide him through his lessons, either? He had no thought of attending university. He didn't seem to know what he wanted to do when he left school. He certainly had no wish to follow in his father's footsteps. He hadn't played the piano in the front room lately, she remembered. She must remind him because she thought he played well. Nicely, she used to say. Perhaps the advent of Jenni had put him off. She hoped not.

At his office in the City Sam was also concerning himself with the problem of Jenni. He could not resist telling his colleagues about it, but he tried to make it clear that it was not his own son he was talking about.

At once one of the men in the office said, 'Oh, I remember a case like that. It was a girl. She had imagined a girl friend called Annie who followed her everywhere. So she said. She even got the family to supply food for her. It wasn't eaten, of course, and eventually the whole thing petered out. The doctor said it was a thing that happened at a certain age.'

'It wears off, does it?' asked Sam.

'Evidently.'

'Your son playing up, Sam?' asked an astute clerk.

'No,' protested Sam. 'The wife's sister was telling me about it.'

'Creatures from outer space. That's what it's all about,' put in someone else.

'I can tell you the parents were very worried about Annie,' continued the first man.

'They must have been,' agreed Sam.

'They were even thinking of going to a shrink.'

'How dreadful for the girl.'

Sam began to regret that he had broached the subject. On the other hand he felt assured that Jon's peculiar fixation might pass. At home he told Mary about the discussion.

'I wish you wouldn't talk about it,' chided Mary.

'I didn't say it was our Jon.'

'People put two and two together.'

'They seemed to think it would pass.'

'I hope it does.'

'Where is he? Upstairs?'

'Yes.'

'Anything happen at school?'

'He didn't say.'

They were sitting in the family sitting room, at the back of the house. The room with the bay window which overlooked the road was known as the front room and it was here that they suddenly heard the piano playing. The old upright piano had belonged to Mary in her youth and she kept it for sentimental reasons.

'That's Jon,' exclaimed Mary.

'I thought you said he was upstairs.'

'He was.'

They listened.

'I must say he plays well,' said Sam. 'Even I have to admit that.'

'He doesn't usually bother with exercises,' commented Mary. 'If they *are* exercises.'

'Sounds as if he's enjoying it, playing about with them.'

Jon was, in fact, turning the piano exercises into variations and embellishing them.

'It's music at school tomorrow. I expect he's getting ready.'

'It sounds different.'

'It does, doesn't it?'

'Jenni again, do you think?'

'Must be. He's never played like that before.'

Jon turned to Jenni as he sat at the piano.

'Is that what you mean?' he asked.

'That's it,' replied Jenni. 'Music doesn't have to be dreary. Enjoy touching the keys. They like being stroked. Think of the piano as a person, a friend.'

'It makes it more interesting, doesn't it?'

'You'll enjoy it.'

'I bet our music teacher, Miss Malloy, would be surprised if she heard us making free with her exercises.'

He left the piano and, taking his piano music with him, went into the sitting room.

'Did you hear that?' he asked.

'Yes,' said Mary. 'What was it?'

'It's in this primer. Jenni thought it would be an idea to improvise on it.'

'It sounded good,' admitted Mary.

'I don't think I'd better try it out on Old Mother Malloy tomorrow,' cried Jon, as he laughed his way upstairs.

'We never had music lessons like that at school,' complained Sam.

'A lot of good it would have done you.'

'I know I'm tone deaf. But I enjoy what the boy plays.'

'I remember,' Mary went on, 'hearing the BBC broadcast to schools. Their music lessons were beyond me.'

'He certainly seems to enjoy his practice now that he's got Jenni to help him.'

'I keep wondering what will happen when she's not there.'

'Yes. I suppose that time will come.'

'We were hoping for just that a little while ago.'

'He'll go back to his bad reports again.'

'I expect so. He's not very good at retaining anything. I wasn't at his age.'

'I don't think I was either. Except for figures, of course, which was more habit than anything.'

The music teacher at Jon's school, Miss Malloy, was a small, fluffy-haired woman of middle age, given to sudden movements when demonstrating something on the piano like some crazed jazzman, bouncing about on the piano stool. To those not keen on music she was a source of amusement. Not so Jon Stern, who listened with interest as Miss Malloy cried, 'Quiet, everyone. I have something to tell you.'

The room became quiet at her request. She went on, 'The Education Authority has inaugurated a piano competition for all schools. It's to be called The Inter-Schools Piano Competition, and any of you who feel like competing should let me know and I'll put their names forward. So hands up anyone who wants to compete.'

There was no movement among the pupils until, after some time, Jon slowly put his hand up.

'You, Jon?' asked Miss Malloy.

'Yes, please, miss.'

'No-one else?'

The room was silent.

'Alright, Jon,' concluded Miss Malloy. 'Come to my office at the end of school and we'll talk about the competition.'

'Thank you, miss.'

* * *

Not very much was heard of Jenni in the Stern household after the music episode. Jon did not tell his parents that he'd put his name down for the Inter-School Competition in case he was rejected before he'd started. Miss Malloy had made it clear that nominations had to be cleared by the Education Authority. Because of the lack of news Sam and Mary even dared to hope that the Jenni obsession was fading out. Either that or Jon was keeping her participation to himself.

Certainly there was nothing to be gained at school by her intervention in such subjects as geography, history or science. She had her opinions, of course, which she voiced to Jon, who tried to ignore them in case he was accused of inattention.

It was during a history lesson, however, that Jon inadvertently raised his voice when answering Jenni, who was suggesting that most history was slanted by propaganda.

The history master, the large, portly Mr Gilbert, looked up and asked, 'What did you say, Stern?'

'Nothing, sir. I didn't say anything.'

'I heard you, boy.'

'I didn't mean to say anything, sir.'

'Were you thinking out loud, perhaps?'

'I must have done. I wasn't aware of it.'

'I heard you use the word "slanted".'

'Did I, sir?'

'Perhaps you could explain. Stand up.'

Jon stood up in front of his desk.

'We're waiting, Stern.'

'Well, sir,' he began, hesitantly, 'I was thinking –'

'I'm pleased to hear it,' commented Mr Gilbert, prompting the inevitable giggles from the rest of the class.

'We're reading about the battle of Agincourt,' explained Jon, 'and Henry the Fifth.'

'That's right.'

'I wondered what it said about it in the French history books.'

'That's what you meant by slanted, is it?'

'Yes, sir.'

'Propaganda, in other words.'

'Yes, sir.'

'Are you a political animal, Stern?'

'No, sir.'

'I don't know what the French history books have to say about it. It would be interesting to find out. Perhaps someone will tell us. Mr Gage, our French tutor, perhaps. Thank you, Stern. Good thinking.'

'Thank you, sir.'

Jon resumed his seat dutifully.

'In the meantime,' Mr Gilbert continued, 'we have to content ourselves with the books that we are given.'

Jon spoke to Jenni in his usual thought-speak.

'You'll get me into trouble.'

'I'll also get you out of it.'

The history lesson proceeded without further interruption. On his way home Jon argued with Jenni.

'Old Gilbert's easy,' he said, 'but if it had been one of the others I could have been in real trouble. I didn't know I'd said anything out loud. We were talking together. It must have slipped out.'

'Aren't you allowed to question history?' Jenni asked.

'No. We have to accept what the books say and what the teachers say.'

'That's a bit one-sided, isn't it?'

'I know. But it's always been like that. There's nothing I can do about it.'

'Or me.'

'That's right. Or you.'

'I'll mind my own business next time.'

'Thank you.'

They laughed together.

'People will think I'm crazy in the head,' admitted Jon, 'walking along the road laughing.'

'Perhaps it will be catching. That would be rather nice.'

Jon was still chuckling to himself as he arrived home. He was met by his mother as usual. They had tea together but with very little conversation. Jon eventually went upstairs to his room. Mary knew better than to question him about events at school.

When Sam arrived home his first thought was about Jenni. Mary shook her head without being asked the question.

'All is quiet,' she whispered.

'Where is he?'

'Upstairs.'

Their attitude appeared to be let sleeping dogs lie. Later in the evening, when they were all together at the dining table, Sam said to Jon, 'I saw your music teacher on the way home.'

'Oh, yes,' said Jon. 'I believe she lives near the station.'

'Funny little thing she is. A gnome of a woman. She's the sort of person you'd expect to be sitting on a stool painting the local church.'

'She's entered me for the Inter-Schools.'

'She's what?' exclaimed Sam, in alarm.

'It's a new thing,' Jon explained. 'The Education Authority or someone has decided to run a piano competition for all schools.'

'And Miss Malloy has put your name up?'

'Yes.'

'She must think a lot of your playing.'

'I suppose so.'

'What with Old Tripp and Miss Malloy, Jon,' said Mary, 'you're doing very well.'

'Thanks to Jenni,' admitted Jon.

Sam and Mary were suddenly silenced, their new-found enthusiasm destroyed, their hope of Jon's progress blighted by something they couldn't understand.

The next thing they knew was that Jon was to be tested as the representative of his school in the competition. The actual progress of testing was taking a long time, as the Examiners were visiting each school that had entered.

'It's my turn today,' said Jon, on the morning of the event.

'That's taken a long time,' remarked Sam.

'They had to test all the entrants, I suppose,' suggested Mary.

'Good luck, anyway,' cried Sam.

'Thank you, Dad. I expect Jenni will help me.'

There it was again, that name, that person.

'Couldn't you do it without her?' asked Sam.

'I don't know, honestly.'

'You shouldn't rely on her all the time,' warned Mary.

'I don't rely on her. She's always there.'

'You're lucky,' put in Sam.

'Yes. I am.'

No more was said. Sam and Mary did not approve of the situation if only because they were certain that Jenni's influence could not last and Jon could be let down. Why should it have started in the first place? They had originally doubted Jenni and all her words but there could be no doubt about the maths ordeal with Mr Tripp or the enthusiasm that Jon was now applying to his music. There was nothing they could do or say. All that they could do was let the situation take its course.

The anxiety was theirs, not Jon's. Jon seemed to take it all in his stride.

Jon was met at the school by Miss Malloy and taken to the music room, where he found himself facing three strange gentlemen of uncertain age. He was not allowed to play anything that he could possibly have prepared but was presented with a folio album that had been made up by the Examiners. Miss Malloy stood beside Jon at the piano to turn the pages.

He could see that the album consisted of rather difficult exercises such as arpeggios and contra-motion as well as scales, of course. Without waiting for anyone to tell him to start, he set about tackling the exercises. He played page after page until he came to the end of the album. Miss Malloy could not believe what she was hearing, for the whole of the album was played without a single wrong note or hesitation. Jon stood up and faced the Examiners.

'Thank you, Stern,' said the Chief Examiner. 'That will be all.'

That was the extent of the competition. Jon gave a short bow and walked out of the room. He resumed his school duties, which, on this occasion, meant Latin with Mr Parker, known as Nosey.

'Ah!' declared Mr Parker as Jon eased himself into his own desk. 'Welcome, Maestro. Perhaps you would care to join us *con brio.*'

Jon opened his book at Caesar's *Gallic Wars*, ignoring the 'Maestro' gibe.

Nothing was heard of the Inter-School Piano Competition for some months, presumably because so many schools had to be visited. And then came the news. Miss Malloy was informed that after careful and thorough scrutiny Jon Stern had emerged top of the competitors. The boy would be presented with a diploma at his own school. There was no suggestion of a revue for an audience or an assembly of competitors. It was simply an announcement as might appear in some government gazette. Miss Malloy immediately informed the Headmaster, who was delighted.

'Have you told Stern?' he asked.

'Not yet,' admitted Miss Malloy.

'Let him know. It's a great feather in our cap. And yours, of course.'

'It certainly is.'

As Miss Malloy was about to leave the room the Headmaster called her back.

'Just a minute, Miss Malloy.'

Miss Malloy returned to the Headmaster's desk.

'On second thoughts,' he said, 'I think the best thing is to announce it at Assembly in the morning. Just don't tell Stern or anybody about it yet.'

'I see. Yes. Alright.'

'Thank you.'

Miss Malloy went out of the room, realising that the Headmaster wanted his little moment of glory. She had hoped to be able to make the announcement herself. It seemed a pity to keep young Stern in suspense, though in all probability he was not expecting to hear anything. He seemed to take the contest in his stride.

Jon was unaware that next morning at Assembly, after prayers, the Headmaster would stand up and say, 'I have an announcement to make.'

He waited while his audience was sufficiently receptive. Then he went on.

'I have some news for you all. In the result of the Inter-Schools Piano Competition this school has come out top.'

There was loud cheering from all the pupils in the hall. When the Headmaster raised his hand for silence he continued, 'For this we are to thank Jon Stern, who will be receiving his diploma from the committee here in due course. Well done, Stern.'

There was renewed cheering with those standing next to Stern patting him on the back. Miss Malloy, who was present on the platform with the other teachers, was surprised that she was not included in the congratulations.

During the remainder of the school day there was a continuous buzz of excitement at the thought of the school becoming famous, to such an extent one of the teachers, in an attempt to call his class to order, declared, 'As far as I'm concerned, it would be music to my ears if I could have your silence.'

Jon himself suffered the adulation of his fellow pupils wherever he went; they seemed to look on him as some previously undiscovered genius. Having survived school, however, and found his way home all that he could bring himself to say was, 'What do you think, Mother? I won that piano competition.'

'Well done!' enthused Mary and threw her arms round him. 'That's against all the other schools, isn't it?' she added.

'Yes.'

'Fantastic. What's the prize?'

'Only a diploma.'

'Still…'

Jon explained during tea time that the official presentation would be at the school.

Sam's attitude, when he was told of the result, was that a cheque would be more useful than a piece of paper. He nevertheless congratulated his son on his achievement.

'Will parents be invited to the presentation?' he asked.

'Depends,' said Jon. 'They may just do it at Assembly.'
'They'll let us know, I suppose.'
'I suppose so.'

The local newspaper covered the presentation at the school one evening, an event to which parents and friends had been invited. There was a certain amount of bunting in the hall, in particular a large version of the school crest draped behind the staff on the platform. All the masters were wearing their gowns, and so was Miss Malloy. Rows and rows of seats filled the hall, with Jon and his mother and father sitting in the front row. The Chief Examiner sat on the platform next to the Head-master. He was not wearing a gown of any kind.

The Headmaster was the first to stand up and speak. He talked about the honour of the school and how proud they all were to have won the competition. He mentioned no names, not even Jon's or Miss Malloy's, until he came to introduce the Chief Examiner, who then stood up and went on about the difficulty of choice, the numbers involved and so on. Eventually he came to the point and presented Jon with the framed diploma. At once there was a burst of applause and Jon left his seat in the front row and climbed the steps that had been set up in front of the platform. He shook hands with the Chief Examiner and then, spontaneously, instinctively, he went across and shook hands with Miss Malloy, who was moved to tears. He then returned to his seat in the hall.

And that was that. There was coffee in the Masters' Common Room for a selected few, which did not include Jon or his parents or any of the pupils. Walking home, Sam couldn't help complaining that he didn't think much of the event. It wouldn't have hurt the school to have laid on refreshments and so on.

'They couldn't have done it for the whole school,' said Mary.

'They could have done it for us and Jon,' suggested Sam. 'After all, he's the star and we're his parents.'

'Forget it, Dad,' declared Jon. 'It's over now. All we need is a hammer and nail to hang this thing on the wall.'

He waved the diploma in the air.

That, in fact, was the first thing Sam did when they reached home. He hung the diploma on the wall in Jon's room and stood back and admired it.

'Thanks, Dad.'

Once on his own Jon called out to Jenni, 'What did you think of all that?'

'Well done.'

'I mean the event.'

'I thought it went very well. I was proud of you.'

'Thank you.'

'I'm glad you went up to Miss Malloy. She'd been a bit neglected.'

'Oh, yes. They froze her out a bit, didn't they?'

'Have you ever considered making a career in music, Jon?'

'A career?' queried Jon, incredulously.

'Yes.'

'You mean like Horowitz and people?'

'Yes.'

'Good Lord.'

'You like music, don't you?'

'Love it.'

'It makes you happy, I've noticed.'

'It does.'

'You could make a lot of other people happy.'

'I'd have to practice a lot.'

'You enjoy it. It's not practice to you. It's still music.'

'I'll have to find some sheet music from somewhere. I'll see if Miss Malloy has any.'

Miss Malloy was surprised when, after a lesson, Jon lingered behind as if he wanted to speak to her.

'Yes, Stern?' she asked.

'Please, miss,' said Jon, 'I want to play a lot of music but I haven't much at home apart from the exercises and a few odd pieces.'

'What do you want to play?'

'Well, all sort of things. Beethoven, Chopin, Liszt.'

'That's very enterprising of you, Stern. I have some here that you could borrow. I'd want it back.'

'Of course, miss.'

'You can take music out of the public library, you know.'

'Can you?'

'You may be underage to join, but your mother and father could be members.'

'I'll tell them.'

'In the meantime, I could take something out for you.'

'Thank you, miss.'

'You really mean to go on with your music, do you?'

'Oh, yes, miss.'

'Very well,' concluded Miss Malloy. 'Come back after school and pick up some of the music I'll leave out for you.'

'Thank you, miss.'

As Jon took himself off, Miss Malloy studied him with mixed feelings. The boy seemed to have taken his music diploma to heart. She knew that he was good at what he had been taught so far, but he obviously wanted to expand. After all, the Inter-Schools was hardly in the category of Musician of the Year or some international competition. It was nothing more than a very advanced examination. There were no sonatas or nocturnes or etudes. She was pleased enough with Jon's enthusiasm but worried about his stability. Could he keep it up? As a scholar he was not noted for his diligence. Whether this was a result of laziness or lack of intelligence no-one could tell. Mr Tripp's recent surprise at the boy's achievement was indicative of Jon's sudden surge of interest in his work, so perhaps he might make something of his music.

The result of Jon's incursion into the world of the classics caused Sam to declare, 'If I hear another mazurka I'll scream.'

'He's getting on very well,' said Mary. 'I like his style, his interpretation.'

'I don't know about that. You can have too much of a good thing.'

The fact was that Jon now spent more time at the piano in the front room than he did in his room upstairs. He was forever playing Miss Malloy's books of Chopin, both the moderate pieces and the difficult ones. He played them until he could commit them to memory. From the Chopin book he turned to the Beethoven sonatas. Sometimes he had to struggle, and to any listener the sound could be excruciating, but he managed it in the end. Every day and as often as possible he played, and far from being exhausted he always came out of the front room feeling refreshed.

On one occasion, Mary said, 'That was a bit of a marathon, wasn't it, dear?'

'I enjoyed it,' replied Jon.

'Bit of a noise,' exclaimed Sam.

Jon sat down with them in the sitting room.

'I like the sound a piano makes,' Jon went on. 'I

45

prefer it to any other instrument. You only have to stroke it and a lovely sound comes out.'

'Is that how Miss Malloy describes it?' asked Mary.

'No,' corrected Jon, 'that's how Jenni describes it.'

Having made the announcement, Jon got up from his chair and went upstairs to his room.

'That bloody woman,' moaned Sam.

'I thought we'd lost her,' said Mary.

'So did I. Just when something's going well he suddenly trots that name out. I could hit him. Or her. What's the matter with the boy? He's nearly seventeen and doesn't know any girls. Does he?'

'I don't think so.'

'He's not one of those, I hope.'

'I'm sure he's not.'

'Don't tell me he's in love with this Jenni non-person.'

'She obviously influences him.'

'Not to the exclusion of the opposite sex, surely.'

'I'm not going to worry about that. As a mother, the longer I can keep him the better.'

'You may rue the day, dear,' Sam laughed.

'I must say I like the way he plays. It's what I would have liked to do but I gave it up.'

'You're not blaming me for that, are you?'

'No. Housekeeping and children are not conducive to a musical career.'

'Career? That's going it a bit.'

'You know what I mean.'

'I used to like those Sunday evenings when you played.'

'Oh, yes. Lloyd Webber and "Yesterday". Now we watch television.'

'Ah!'

Sam's exclamation said it all. Everything stopped for television.

46

'You know, dear,' Sam went on, 'It's time Jon started thinking of a career. He'll be leaving school in twelve months.'

'I don't think he'll follow you into accountancy,' warned Mary.

'No. I've given up on that dream.'

'Have you ever spoken to him about a career?'

'No. I'd better, I suppose.'

The opportunity occurred sooner than Sam anticipated. Instead of him tackling his son about his intentions, Jon tackled his father and his mother together.

'Dad,' he began one evening, 'the Headmaster had some of us in today to ask us what we wanted to do as a career.'

'Oh,' said Sam, nonplussed. 'What did you tell him?'

'I said I wanted to do something connected with music.'

'Music?' repeated Sam, incredulously.

'Yes.'

'What, for God's sake? Music is a hobby.'

'Not necessarily.'

'What then?'

'There's no need to get worked up, dear,' soothed Mary.

'I'm not getting worked up,' cried Sam. 'I just don't know what the boy means. Does he mean playing the piano in some night club?'

'I think you'll find he means concert work.'

'You mean play in the Albert Hall? That sort of thing?'

'Well...' Mary didn't know what to say.

'Some hope!' exclaimed Sam.

'It's all I want to do,' protested Jon.

'Well, you'll have to think of something else,' concluded Sam.

'What?' queried Jon. 'What else?'

'I don't know,' complained Sam. 'You don't want accountancy.'

'Heaven forbid!' cried Jon.

'You'd better consult a careers adviser. There are such people. There's the law, for instance.'

'I don't fancy that,' said Jon.

'You don't know what you do fancy,' complained Sam.

'I'm going to play!' exclaimed Jon, somewhat petulantly.

He went into the front room and shut the door.

'Mary!' cried Sam, in desperation. 'What are we going to do?'

'Leave it, dear,' advised Mary. 'There's time yet. He's still got another year at school after this. Something might turn up.'

'You think the music idea might be forgotten?'

'I suggest we wait and see.'

'I feel so bloody helpless,' moaned Sam.

'I must say he's an exceptional pianist,' admitted Mary.

'So are a lot of people who happen to do ordinary jobs at the same time.'

'Oh, I know.'

Mary really wanted to go on to say that she was convinced that her own son was potentially of concert standard. So it was left that Mary had her own hopes while Sam was sure that his son would never amount to anything worthwhile.

Jon could not sleep very well that night. He was worried about the future. His father had unnerved him and made all his dreams come crashing to the ground. Admittedly they were only dreams, but to Jon they were real. Music had become important to him, it had entered his very being. He wanted to play and keep on playing. It was all he ever wanted to do and it worried him because his father wanted him to have a career which had nothing to do with music. A voice came to him as he was tossing and turning in bed.

'What are you worried about, Jon?' asked Jenni.

Jon sat up suddenly.

'Jenni!' he answered eagerly.

'I can tell you're worried.'

'It's this music business.'

'What about it?'

'I want to keep it up. Even after school.'

'Why shouldn't you?'

'I don't know how to go about it. Neither does Dad. In fact he's dead against it.'

'You could try Miss Malloy. She should be able to help you.'

'She should. I wonder if she could. I'll talk to her.'

'Tell her how you feel.'

'I will.'

With yet another new dream to think about, Jon turned over and went to sleep.

The piano in the Stern front room was now being used more than ever. Instead of staying upstairs and playing with his computer and such paraphernalia as young boys acquired, Jon would go into the front room immediately after his tea and stay there until Mary called him for their evening meal.

Jon's eagerness got him into trouble with Miss Malloy. Delighted as she was with his progress and impressed as she was with his application, she had to reprimand him for taking too much upon himself in his capacity of star pupil in the music room. Before the commencement of the music class, when the pupils were sitting about waiting for Miss Malloy to arrive, Jon decided to sit at the school piano and amuse himself. He indulged in scales, chromatics, contra-motion and all the intricate exercises in the book.

'He's only showing off,' said the Lacey boy.

'Thinks he's bloomin' Chopin,' said another.

'That's enough!' commanded Miss Malloy as she strode into the room.

Jon slipped off the piano stool quickly and took his place in the class.

'This piano,' continued Miss Malloy, 'is only to be used with my permission – and that applies to you, Stern, as it does to everybody else. Is that understood?'

'Yes, miss,' muttered Jon, penitently.

Because of the reprimand Jon decided that it was not a good time to ask Miss Malloy about his future.

In spite of her admonitions, however, Miss Malloy had great aspirations for her star pupil. She was convinced that he had a rare talent.

'That boy's got something,' she would declare in the Masters' Common Room when she was with the rest of the teaching staff.

'You've got a thing about that boy,' chided one of the teachers. 'Not so long ago you were calling him too laid-back for his own good.'

'I know,' she admitted. 'It's a complete turn-about.'

'I had an example of that a little while ago,' put in Mr Tripp. 'He surprised me with a difficult equation. Never thought he'd break it.'

'I've a good mind to enter him for the Young Musician of the Year,' enthused Miss Malloy.

'You mean that thing you see on the BBC?' asked Mr Tripp.

'Yes.'

'You must be mad,' exclaimed one of the teachers.

'How are you going to do that?' asked another.

50

'I don't know,' admitted Miss Malloy, 'but I'll find out.'

'There must be hundreds of entries for that,' suggested Mr Tripp.

'I'm sure,' agreed Miss Malloy. 'But I expect they have auditions to whittle the numbers down.'

Before she said anything to Jon himself or his parents, the diminutive Miss Malloy pestered the BBC to find out about the application routine. As she suspected, there were auditions before any candidate was allowed to be accepted as a competitor. Local auditions would be held in London in the summer, followed by several other rounds at intervals.

Once she had discovered as much as necessary for her purpose, she approached Jon Stern at the end of one of her music classes when the rest of the class had been dismissed.

'Stern,' she said, 'how do you feel about going in for another competition?'

'I don't mind, miss.'

'I'm talking about Young Musician of the Year. You've probably seen it televised by the BBC.'

'Ooer!' cried Jon, with a laugh.

'I'd like to submit your name.'

'Shouldn't I ask my father first, miss?'

'Of course. Ask him and tell me what he says.'

'He's not very interested in music. You may have to explain it to him.'

'I will, if necessary.'

'I'll tell him tonight.'

'Good. Tell him it will mean auditions in London over a few days.'

'I will, miss.'

'Alright, Stern. Off you go.'

'Miss.'

Jon hurried out of the room in order to catch up with

his next lesson. When he arrived home he told his mother what Miss Malloy had said about Young Musician of the Year.

'What?' exclaimed Mary, in alarm. 'You mean where someone plays the violin, someone else plays the clarinet? That sort of thing?'

'Yes.'

'The thing we see on television?'

'Yes.'

'How do we go about that?' asked Mary, more calmly.

'Miss Malloy wants to organise it, if you agree.'

'Where would all this happen?'

'The auditions would be in London, she says.'

'Oh dear. Heaven knows what your father is going to say.'

'He wouldn't stand in the way, would be?'

'In the way of what?'

'Well, my career, I suppose.'

'That's what I'm afraid of. He doesn't call it a career.'

'The winner gets a cheque. You've seen that on television.'

'That might help.'

'You wouldn't stand in the way yourself, would you?'

'Of course not. But I'm not your father. '

'Miss Malloy is prepared to talk to him.'

'She may have to,' concluded Mary.

The house had been transformed as a result of Jon's enthusiasm. He never seemed to be away from the piano. Sam found it getting on his nerves and this particular evening he was in a complaining mood.

'Why does he keep playing the same thing over and over?' he asked, petulantly.

'He's trying to learn it.'

'But he knows it. He's got the music there.'

'He's trying to memorise it.'

52

'Why?'

'You can't play in public with music on the stand.'

'Why not?'

'You can't. You just can't.'

'Play in public, did you say?'

'Yes.'

'When?'

'Miss Malloy wants him to enter for the Young Musician of the Year.'

'Over my dead body.'

'It's an honour, dear.'

'Honour nothing. It's going too far. Playing for pleasure is one thing, but trying to make a career out of it…'

'Miss Malloy obviously thinks he has a future.'

'Miss Malloy is only a school teacher.'

'You wouldn't stand in his way, would you, dear?'

'The boy's only seventeen. You're talking as if he's bloody Horowitz or somebody.'

'Just the right age for Young Musician of the Year.'

'Are you serious?'

'Yes. It's a wonderful chance for him if he gets through the audition.'

'What audition?'

'Evidently they hold auditions to pare down the numbers.'

'Where?'

'In London.'

'When?'

'That I don't know. Miss Malloy could tell us.'

'I don't like the sound of any of this. It's taking Jon away from his lessons.'

'It's during the holidays.'

'Oh, is it? You've really gone into it, haven't you? You're in favour, I suppose.'

'I'd like to see the boy achieve something.'

'Piano playing!' scoffed Sam.

'He could become famous.'

'Don't make me laugh.'

'You've heard him.'

'Yes, I know. He sounds good. But so do a lot of other people.'

'He's good and he's different. Why don't you just drop Miss Malloy a line saying you approve and he can take it to her in the morning. It doesn't commit you to anything.

'I'll admit I'm out of my depth.'

'Poor Sam.'

'You think a letter would be enough?'

'Oh, yes.'

Mary did not want her husband to indulge in too much discussion with Miss Malloy in case she put him off. She saw the possibility of Musician of the Year as a showcase for Jon, presuming, of course, in her maternal allegiance, that he would pass the heats. She also presumed, wrongly as it happened, that the winner would automatically become a concert pianist. She wasn't quite sure logistically how that was achieved. She had no idea how a pianist came to play at the Royal Albert Hall, for instance, or any other hall, come to that, but she hoped that one day Jon might aspire to it.

Jon duly presented Miss Malloy with his father's letter, which she opened in front of him after the music lesson.

'Oh, lovely!' she exclaimed. 'Now we must get down to work.'

As a result of Jon getting down to work, Sam's hearing was assaulted by a barrage of what he called 'that bloody thing', which happened to be a Rachmaninoff prelude that Jon was preparing for his audition. He played it over and over at the least opportunity, not only to

54

commit it to memory but to fine tune it in his own fashion. He wanted to make sure that familiarity did not breed indifference and make the piece sound automatic.

'That would sound wonderful on a concert grand,' said Mary one evening.

'That's all we need,' moaned Sam.

'It's a very difficult piece.'

'Why doesn't he play something easier?'

'He wants to impress the judges.'

'More likely frighten them.'

Evidently the auditions were spread over several days and it would be necessary for Jon to go to London each day, as it was not possible to nominate times.

'He can't go up to London every day,' cried Sam. 'Think of the fares!'

'I know. I thought of that.'

'Can't they let him know when he's wanted?'

'They say they can't.'

'Why not?'

'I don't know, dear. I'm not in charge.'

'It's all very well. It's not as if you can be sure of the result. I told you it was only an ego trip.'

'I wonder if Louise would put him up?'

'Your sister?'

'Yes.'

'We haven't spoken to her for ages.'

'You haven't. I have.'

'Why don't you ask her?'

'I will.'

'Go on, then.'

'I'll wait till I'm on my own.'

'Why?'

'I'll have to build up to it. I can't just thrust it on her.'

Sam grunted something that Mary did not understand.

Once Jon was at school and Sam had left for the office, Mary telephoned her sister.

'Mary!' cried Louise. 'What a surprise!'

'I'm afraid it is,' said Mary.

'What do you mean?'

'I have a problem.'

'Who hasn't?'

'No. I'm serious.'

'What have you done now?' asked Louise, ominously.

'It's not me. It's Jon!'

'Oh. Yes?'

'His music teacher at the school has put him up for Young Musician of the Year.'

'How wonderful!'

'Well, it is and it isn't. He has to attend a certain number of auditions in London and they can't say which days.'

'Typical.'

'Sam's not keen on all the fares for what he thinks is a waste of time.'

'Typical again.'

'I wonder if you could put him up.'

'Of course, dear. Only too pleased. It will be company for Pam.'

'How is she?'

'Fine. She did think of applying to the Royal Academy of Music, but then she doesn't want to make a career of the piano, so why go through all that?'

'She and Jon are a pair. Music mad.'

'She'll be thrilled when I tell her Jon's up for Musician of the Year.'

'It's only an audition.'

'That's not to be sneezed at.'

'I could pay you something for his board.'

'You'll do nothing of the sort!'

'That's very kind of you. Sam will be relieved.'

'I couldn't care less about that, as you know.'

'I know.'

'Just let me know when the boy's coming, dear.'

'I will. And thanks, Louise.'

Louise Martin lived in a spacious apartment in Manchester Square just off Marylebone High Street. It was on the first floor of the building with sufficient accommodation for Jon to have his own bedroom and bathroom.

He arrived in the afternoon, having walked from Charing Cross with his small suitcase. He had studied a map of the streets of London with his father the evening before. Nevertheless he found it necessary to ask the way once or twice.

Arriving at the building in Manchester Square, Jon mounted the stone steps to the front entrance which consisted of double mahogany doors, highly polished, beside which a panel of buttons displayed the names of the residents. Jon pressed the button named Martin. As he waited a voice beside the panel said, 'Who is it?'

Jon put his face to the panel and said, 'It's me, Auntie. Jon.'

'Jon!' cried Louise. 'Come right up.' There was the sound of a click and Jon was able to push the heavy front door open. He stood facing a wide staircase carpeted in a dark red pattern. He started to climb. The house was very quiet, not even the noise of the traffic outside penetrated the building. On the first floor landing there were three more mahogany doors and each displayed a brass plate proclaiming the name of the occupant. Before he could read any of the names the door at the end of the landing opened and there stood Aunt Louise, a large blonde lady with arms outstretched in a welcome.

'Jon!' she cried. 'Come here!'

She enveloped him in her ample bosom and hugged him.

'Hello, Aunt,' muttered Jon.

'Come in. Come in,' urged Louise, propelling Jon into the apartment.

Jon looked about himself as his aunt closed the front door. He was impressed by the surroundings. There was an expensive air about them. He knew that his mother's sister was fairly well off. He had heard it mentioned at home and this was evidence of it. Her husband had died and left her a lot of money and she lived in this luxurious apartment with her daughter, Pam.

'Would you like a cup of tea, dear?' asked Louise.

'Yes, please,' replied Jon.

'Let me show you to your room first then you can freshen up while I'm making it.'

Louise led the way along a dark corridor between the sitting room and the bedrooms. Jon's was to be a small room with a single bed but there was a bathroom and toilet next door. These were things that Jon was certainly not used to and were rather overwhelming, making him feel a little inferior, the poor relation. He put his suitcase on the bed and took out his toilet bag. He wanted to wash his hands, which was something of a fetish with him as he liked to associate clean hands with the piano keys. He then made his way back to the sitting room where his Aunt Louise was waiting for him with the tea laid out.

'Come on, dear,' she called. 'You must be dying for a cup after your journey.'

He was invited to sit at the table, which, he noticed, was laid out for three people.

'Thank you,' said Jon, shyly.

'Sugar and milk?'

'Yes, please.'

Jon noticed that his aunt did not put the milk in first as his mother did.

'We won't wait for Pam. She went to the cinema. She knows you're coming.'

'Where's the piano, Auntie?'

'In the drawing room.'

'Oh.'

'It's a Bluthner grand.'

'Oh.'

'Pam adores it. Her father gave it to her on her sixteenth birthday.'

'Oh.'

'Help yourself to the sandwiches, dear.'

'Thank you.'

He reached out and took what he presumed was a paste sandwich of some sort, avoiding the more obvious cucumber in case the filling fell out. Aunt Louise handed him a plate and a paper napkin, so he was expected to put the sandwich on the plate before eating it.

At home he would have eaten it straight away without the use of a plate. The sandwich was half-way to his mouth when he heard the front door bang shut and a female voice call out, 'I'm home!'

'Ah!' cried Louise. 'There she is.'

The next thing Jon knew, an attractive girl burst into the room. She had Jet black hair cut into a bob with a fringe, an oval face with dark eyes and brows, an inviting mouth touched with red lipstick. She was Jon's height with long legs and a full bosom. This was his cousin Pam, whom he had not seen for some years but had always remembered with affection. She stopped dead at the sight of him.

'Jon!' she screamed.

Jon stood up and politely held out his hand.

'Hello, Pam.'

Ignoring the proffered hand, Pam put her arms round his neck and embraced him warmly.

'The last time I saw you you were in short pants,' she declared.

'Yes,' laughed Jon. 'I don't remember what kind of pants you were wearing.'

'I should hope not.'

'Come and sit down and have your tea,' urged Louise.

'So,' exclaimed Pam, helping herself to a sandwich without using a plate. 'You've got an audition for Musician of the Year.'

'Yes. I'm dreading it.'

'Don't. You'll be alright. Won't he, Mother?'

'Of course,' agreed Louise.

'I'm told there could be more than one audition,' explained Jon. 'If I'm only called for one I presume I'm out. If I'm called for more than one I'm in with a chance.'

'Don't worry,' said Pam. 'We'll play after tea to get you in trim.'

'Oh, good.'

'When I knew you were coming I popped up the road and got some duets.'

'That's an idea.'

Aunt Louise, unable to join in the conversation, sat beaming at the two musical enthusiasts.

'We only have an old upright at home,' admitted Jon.

'Much tidier,' said Pam. 'Grands take up a lot of room. Who's your favourite composer?'

'Schubert.'

'Me too. Just as good as Beethoven and a nicer person, I always think.'

'Certainly gentler.'

'He never had as much help as Beethoven.'

'Help?'

'Financially. Beethoven always had sponsors. When one of them lost everything in a fire he said, "What about my money?" Poor old Schubert never had anyone to keep him while he worked.'

'I didn't know that about Beethoven.'

'It's in one of the biographies I read.'

'Could I borrow it?'

'Sure.'

Jon was completely captivated by his cousin. He had had little or no contact with the opposite sex. They had never really interested him. Apart from a few casual acquaintances in his own neighbourhood, he had always been a loner. At school he was aware that some of the boys had taken up with some of the girls but none of them had appealed to him. They had been bright scholars, brighter than he, but they had no conversation beyond cosmetics, clothes and hairdressing. But here, with his cousin, he was face to face not only with a very attractive girl in the physical sense but one with an air of assured sophistication and a knowledge of music, all of which intrigued him. He would like to be like her, he decided. He assumed that it was the result of living in London. By comparison he was a country bumpkin.

After tea Pam suggested that she should introduce Jon to her piano, so they both left the table and went into the drawing room, leaving Louise to clear away the tea things, which she did to the accompaniment of the music coming from the other room. She knew that it was not her own daughter playing. It wasn't her style, her touch. She stopped in her work to listen. There was something about the playing that intrigued her. It wasn't the music but the way it was played. There was something different about it that gave a new sound to a familiar tune.

In the drawing room Jon was sitting at the piano with Pam standing by his side. He was playing a Chopin prelude and when he finished he looked up and said, 'Lovely piano. Not easy to keep quiet.'

'You know,' said Pam, contemplatively, 'it's a funny thing. I don't know what it is but you make the music mean something.'

'Do I? How?'

'I don't know. Let me play it.'

Jon moved along the wide piano stool to let Pam sit down beside him. She began to play the music that he had just played.

In the kitchen Louise heard the piece being played again and could tell the difference. She knew that it was her daughter playing. When she had finished Pam turned to Jon.

'Not the same, is it?'

'Well, it's your way.'

'But I prefer your way. How do I do it?'

'I don't know.'

'Play it again.'

They changed places on the piano stool and Jon played the prelude again. He did not play in exactly the same way, although he himself was unaware of any change. It was a habit of his. He admitted that he never played a piece of music the same way every time. It depended how he felt.

'That was slightly different,' said Pam.

'Yes,' agreed Jon. 'I don't seem to be able to play a piece the same way every time. I just play it how I feel. It's like a sweet. You want it to last and you want to enjoy sucking it.'

'I'm inclined to swallow the sweet whole. That's

familiarity, I suppose. You just play and that's that. Like some perfectionists. It's just a job to them. You put your fingers in the right place at the right time and that's that.'

'You said you had some duets we could play.'

'Oh, yes. I've got the *Dolly Suite* somewhere.'

Pam went to the music cabinet and searched through the drawers for the music.

'Here we are,' she announced, waving the book in her hand.

They sat together on the piano stool and played Bizet's *Dolly Suite*, Pam taking the secondo and Jon the primo.

On her way back from the kitchen Aunt Louise heard the sound and was so curious about it that she went into the drawing room and stood watching the two young people so obviously enjoying themselves playing together and laughing as they came to the end of the score, proud of their achievement. Aunt Louise could not help noticing how well the two of them got on together. She thought they made an attractive pair and, being a mother, wondered if they would become a couple. She had to admit that Jon was by no means as worldly-wise as her daughter, but no doubt Pam would be able to cure that. Unless Jon made a success of his piano playing he was no financial catch, of course. Pam, she knew, had no regular boyfriend, attractive as she was, so she could not help contemplating a pleasant relationship between the two cousins. But the likelihood was that Jon would go back to his little suburban house and the two would be unlikely to meet again.

Just as Jon was fascinated by his cousin's behaviour and demeanour, Pam, in turn, was captivated by Jon's lack of sophistication and his very naivety. This became apparent later that evening. Aunt Louise always sat down to dinner at eight o'clock, sometimes alone if Pam happened to be out. On this occasion she was joined by Pam and Jon.

She need not have worried. Her mind was made up for her, though she was unaware of it, for that night when they all went to bed Louise took her sleeping pill as usual. It was something she'd been doing since her husband died. Consequently Pam was able to creep along the corridor to Jon's room without fear of detection. She knocked on the door.

'Come in,' called Jon, completely unaware of who might be knocking in the middle of the night.

The door opened and Pam came in, wearing a revealing pale blue pyjama suit.

'Can I come in?' she whispered.

'You are in,' said Jon, sitting up in the bed.

'Am I disturbing you?' she asked.

'No. I'm pleased to see you.'

'Are you?'

'Of course.'

'I hope your auditions take a long time.'

'So do I. Now.'

There was an embarrassing silence between them as they gazed at each other in anticipation.

'Am I keeping you awake?' asked Pam.

'No. I'm not sleepy.'

'Neither am I.'

There was another silence until Pam asked, 'Can I get in there with you?'

'Yes. Of course,' said Jon, throwing back the bedding to create an opening for Pam to nestle in beside him. They were then both sitting up in bed.

'It's warm in here, isn't it?' remarked Pam.

'I didn't open the window because of the traffic noise. Shall I open it?'

64

'No. I'll take this jacket off.'

Pam unbuttoned her pyjama jacket and slipped it off her shoulders. Jon was left admiring the girl's full round breasts.

'They're nice.'

'Thank you.'

'Aren't you worried about your mother?'

'No. She'll sleep like the dead till eight o'clock. She takes a pill.'

'Oh.'

'Why don't you take your jacket off?' suggested Pam.

'What? Yes. Why not?'

When they were both naked to the waist Pam said, 'That's better.'

She turned and nestled against Jon's naked chest, at the same time putting her hand down under the bedclothes to find Jon's already erect penis, which she could feel through his thin pyjama trousers.

'That's what I call forte,' said Pam, causing both of them to chuckle and embrace, kissing eagerly, tongues entwined. It was Jon's first experience of such intercourse and he was quite happy to lose his virginity, particularly with his favourite cousin.

'I'd better leave you to get some sleep,' said Pam, eventually.

'Do you have to go?' pleaded Jon, nuzzling her breasts.

'No. We can both sleep here.'

'Let's do that.'

'That is, if you let me sleep and save your fingers for the piano.'

And so the two cousins slept in each other's arms that night. Pam crept out of the room in the early morning while Jon was still asleep.

At breakfast next morning the two behaved as if

nothing had happened. Both by word and gesture they were able to allay Aunt Louise's suspicions.

'Did you sleep well, Jon?' she asked.

'Yes, thank you, Aunt,' replied Jon. 'I had a lovely night.'

The remark was not lost on Pam, who, looking down at her plate, grinned happily.

'I hope all goes well today,' said Louise.

'They may not get to me today,' admitted Jon. 'I don't know how many are up for the auditions.'

'Never mind,' said Pam. 'You can come back here until they call you. Can't he, Mother?'

'Of course,' confirmed Aunt Louise.

The auditions were convened at the BBC Television Centre and when Jon made his way there he was not surprised to see a long queue, which he joined. From what he could gather of the talk around him, the queue consisted of instrumentalists of all kinds, not only the piano. When he eventually shuffled to his place at the head of the queue with many contestants still behind him, he was asked for details, which he was able to supply and then, the final question: type of instrument, to which he was able to answer: piano. It was the luck of the draw which instrument came first, which, in turn, would determine the duration of the auditions. He was told to take his place in the crush. Eventually some kind of official came to announce that a programme had been devised, and accordingly piano competitors would be called in two days' time. Jon slunk away and began to make his way back to his Aunt Louise's apartment.

'What do you think of that, Jenni?' he mused as he wandered along.

'Only to be expected,' said Jenni.

'I'll have to ring Mother and tell her I'm staying at Pam's.'

'Pam won't mind,' remarked Jenni.

'No. She's nice, isn't she?'

'Very.'

Jon noticed that Jenni made no comment about their behaviour in the bedroom. Perhaps she didn't notice that sort of thing. He decided not to mention it. By the time he made his way back to Manchester Square it was nearly tea time. The door was opened by Pam herself.

'How did it go?' she asked, eagerly.

'Two days,' said Jon.

'Oh, good. That means we can play together. I went out and bought some more duet albums.'

By the time they reached the sitting room Louise came from her bedroom where she'd been resting.

'How did it go, dear?' she asked.

'He's got to wait two days, Mother,' said Pam.

'Oh, what a shame.'

'I must ring Mother,' said Jon.

'You do that, dear, and Pam and I will get the tea.'

'It's a bit early, Mother,' Pam pointed out.

'Four o'clock,' said Louise. 'Everything stops for tea. Remember?'

Jon telephoned his mother.

'I've got to wait a couple of days, Mother.'

'Oh, dear. Does your aunt mind?'

'No. She seems quite keen. Until I start practising, I expect.'

'She should be used to it with Pam.'

'We've been playing duets.'

'Oh, good. Give them my love.'

'I will. See you, Mother.'

'Yes, dear.'

Jon rang off and returned to the sitting room.

While they were all at tea, Jon said, 'I'm afraid I'm going to have to bore you all with my practice for the audition. I daren't let up.'

'Oh, we won't mind that,' declared Louise.

'The Rachmaninoff and the Liszt, isn't it, Jon?' asked Pam.

'Yes. I told you. Two contrasting pieces.'

'I like the quiet one,' said Louise.

'That's the Liszt,' explained Pam.

Jon filled his time in until he was due to audition by playing and playing and playing. Pam was surprised at his perseverance. He deserved to win, she thought. She noticed that in spite of the repetition his playing still sounded new, never stale. She was afraid that repetition would blunt his enthusiasm by the time it came to his audition.

Jon made his way once more to the venue for the audition. Pam and Louise wished him good luck as he set off. He still had to wait about, though. He was told that he might not be called until the afternoon, but still he sat waiting. He could hear other competitors playing and, to him, they all sounded excellent and his spirits began to fall. Eventually he was called upon to perform before three judges whom he did not recognise and to whom he bowed slightly before sitting at the piano. Once his fingers touched the keys he forgot all about queues and waiting, all about the idea of any competition. He simply lost himself. He didn't even notice that the judges turned to each other in some surprise as he played, a gesture that could suggest either success or failure. At the end of it all he was told that he would be advised in due course. So he left.

Once again he arrived at Manchester Square at tea time to the usual question: 'How did you get on?'

'They'll let me know,' Jon told them. 'You'll be advised, as they called it.'

'Right,' said Louise, sharply. 'Tea.'

'That's Mother's answer to everything,' explained Pam. 'Tea.'

'I must get off home,' said Jon.

'Oh, no!' moaned Pam.

'Mother will be expecting me and I mustn't outstay my welcome here.'

'You could never do that,' said Pam.

The two cousins were in the sitting room while Aunt Louise was arranging tea.

'I'll miss you, Jon,' said Pam.

'I'll miss you, too,' admitted Jon.

'I wish you were nearer.'

'So do I.'

'I'm supposed to do my last year at school but I don't fancy it.'

'You're not a schoolboy. You're a pianist.'

'Try telling Dad that.'

'Tea!' called Louise, from the kitchen.

'I'll pack after tea,' said Jon, as they both made their way to the kitchen.

Tea time was a subdued event. Louise tried to make bright conversation but the two cousins were too depressed to appreciate her efforts. When Jon left the kitchen to pack his suitcase Louise said: 'It's been nice having him, hasn't it?'

'Very.'

'I'll miss him.'

Pam did not trust herself to answer lest she should burst into tears. Then Jon appeared in the doorway with his suitcase.

'Well,' he announced, 'thank you for putting up with me, Aunt.'

'It was a pleasure, dear,' declared Louise, giving the boy a kiss on the cheek.

Jon held out his hand.

'Goodbye, Pam.'

'I'll see you off,' said Pam, abruptly, ignoring the proffered hand.

Louise stayed in the kitchen as Pam led the way to the front door. Pam and Jon went down the stairs together to the main door at street level, where they hugged each other gently. Pam was rather tearful and Jon had to admit that he had a lump in his throat.

'I shall feel lonely in bed tonight,' said Pam, with a brave chuckle.

'So shall I,' admitted Jon.

'Ring me sometimes,' whispered Pam.

'I will.'

Pam stood on the steps waving until Jon turned the corner out of sight. She still stood there briefly before returning to her apartment.

'Have you been crying?' asked Louise, in surprise, when Pam came in.

'No. Of course not,' protested Pam, turning towards her bedroom.

Louise watched her daughter turn away. She frowned. Had the girl fallen in love with her cousin? It was possible. He was a nice-looking boy, in no way sophisticated, but that could have its own appeal. She decided not to question the girl. Let it take its own course.

Sitting in the corner of the carriage on his way home Jon wondered how, even after such a short visit, he could return to the humdrum life of his suburban home. It was his home, nevertheless. He couldn't desert his mother. His father was different. He knew he didn't approve of all this music business, as he was inclined to call it. Jon wasn't too sure himself about the future. Now, more than ever, he wanted to immerse himself in music.

'Jenni,' he whispered. 'What shall I do?'

'Nothing.'

'What do you mean, nothing?'

'Just let things happen. They'll sort themselves out.'

'Will they? I enjoyed being with Pam, by the way.'

'So I noticed.'

Jon didn't know what to make of Jenni's enigmatic remark. If she was as omnipresent as she suggested, then she must have been aware of their sexual exploits. Perhaps they attached no significance to such things. Jon decided not to pursue the conversation and said no more for the remainder of the journey.

Arriving home, Jon was greeted by his mother as if he'd been away for months. It was near dinner time.

'Darling!' cried Mary excitedly.

'Hello, Mother.'

Once they'd progressed to the kitchen Mary said, 'Take your things upstairs. We'll have something to eat when your father gets here.'

'Right.'

Jon heaved his suitcase up the narrow staircase. When he came downstairs again, he said, 'It's strange being back. I can't get used to it.'

'You'll come down to earth in a minute,' predicted Mary.

'It's another world.'

'What is?'

'This.'

'You've lived here all your life so far. It shouldn't be strange.'

'London is so different.'

'Of course it is. I couldn't live there. Neither could your father. That's why we live here.'

'I think I could live in London.'

'Well, naturally. If you want to be a concert pianist you've got to be in the scene.'

'It's a nice flat Aunt Louise's got.'

'Yes?'

'Have you been there?'

'Not for a long time. When your Uncle John was alive.'

'I never met him.'

'You did but you were too small.'

There was a lull in the conversation. Mary sensed that Jon wanted to talk more about Aunt Louise.

'Are they very rich?' he asked.

'I wouldn't say that. Her husband left her comfortably off.'

'They don't live like us.'

'I don't suppose they do. My sister always had fanciful ideas.'

'They have a grand piano.'

'I'm sure.'

'I played some duets with Pam.'

'Did you?'

'She's very good.'

'You enjoyed it then?'

'Very much.'

'Well, I don't suppose you'll be going again.'

'No?'

'There won't be any reason, will there?'

'No. I suppose not.'

Jon was crestfallen and confused. He wanted to be part of the life that included Pam. He would like to have phoned her but he was loath to do so in front of his mother and so soon after leaving the girl. He didn't have a mobile and couldn't use a phone box because he had no cause to go out. Besides, he didn't have any money. He would have to reverse the charges, which he was sure Pam would do. He was dreading the arrival of his father because he knew he would be asked a lot of questions he couldn't answer about the competition. He was also worried about school next term. He wanted to leave school and concentrate on music. He wondered if he could get a scholarship to the Royal Academy. That would be near Pam. Perhaps he could stay with her while he was at the Academy. According to Miss Malloy, you stay for three years. And then what? As his father would say: What then? How do you go about getting a job? What would he do for wages? He couldn't play in an orchestra because he only had the piano. He could only play in pubs and clubs. He couldn't imagine his father putting up with that. He wanted more than that for himself, anyway.

When Sam arrived home he was glad to see his son, of course, but couldn't resist wanting to know what would happen next. Nobody could tell him because they all had to wait. But Jon couldn't resist making a statement.

'I don't want to go back to school next term, Dad,' he said.

'Oh dear,' muttered Mary. 'I'm afraid you'll have to, son,' declared Sam.

'Why?'

'Because you've got to complete your education. That's why.'

'Why couldn't I go to the Royal Academy of Music?'

'What do they do?'

'You study for three years.'

'And how much is that likely to cost?'

'I could get a scholarship.'

'You mean try. And if you fail?'

'It's too much of a risk, Jon,' suggested Mary.

'What can they do for you after the three years? Get you a job in a hotel bar?'

'No. Oh, I don't know,' cried Jon in exasperation, running out of the room.

'Poor boy,' said Mary.

'I think he's got ideas above his station. Either he has or Miss Malloy has.'

'Although I said it was a risk, I'm pretty sure he'd gain a scholarship to the Academy.'

'He's got to live at the same time. Even if he goes to and fro he's got to have fare and food.'

'I'm sure that Louise would put him up.'

'For three years?'

'I see what you mean.'

During a calm moment, following the discussion about the Academy, Sam remarked, 'He hasn't said anything about Jenni lately, has he?'

'No,' replied Mary. 'She seems to have been forgotten.'

'Thank Heaven for that.'

'Oh, it wasn't so bad. She did help him, remember.'

'That's true. There is that.'

They were not to know that at that point in their conversation Jon was actually pouring his heart out to Jenni.

'It's so frustrating, Jenni,' he cried.

'I told you not to worry.'

'How can I help it, with Dad saying I have to go back to school next term?'

'Everything depends on the result of your audition.'

'I haven't any great hopes of that.'

'Why not?'

'There were so many competitors. They must all be good or they wouldn't have been put up for it.'

'The same thing happened with the Inter-Schools. You won that.'

'These people are much older. None of them looked as if they went to school.'

'More credit to you.'

'It was only an audition. I had to go through with that because Miss Malloy put me up.'

'There's only one thing to do now then.'

'What's that?'

'Practise, practise, practise.'

'Right,' said Jon, quite emphatically.

True to his word Jon spent most of his time practising. He practised for hours on end. Mary was glad enough to have her son at home all day, as happened during school holidays, but she wished that sometimes he would ease up on his practice. When she suggested it he said, 'It's not practice, Mother. It's work. I should do eight hours a day at least.'

When the weather was warm enough Mary opened the windows of the front room and she was gratified to notice a little group of people lingering on the pavement to listen to the music.

Apart from the hours of earnest practice, Mary noticed that Jon was spending quite a lot of time on the telephone talking to his cousin Pam. As far as she could make out the conversation was mostly about music, but the tone of voice and the long pauses suggested some kind of intimacy between them. She wasn't worried. She was pleased. She was very fond of her niece.

Mary was the first to notice the little 'BBC' on the envelope as it fell on the mat in the hall. She picked it up and looked at it. Jon was still upstairs. So was Sam. It was early morning and she was preparing breakfast for them all. She took the mail into the kitchen and put the letters by the individual plates; Sam's on his plate and the single BBC one on Jon's. Sam was down before Jon and sat and opened his letters. He noticed the letter on Jon's plate.

'What's that?' he asked.

'Can't you tell? Look at the initials.'

'Oh, dear. I hope he's prepared for a disappointment.'

'Don't say anything.'

'I won't.'

They were both eating when Jon came down to face his bacon and eggs. He looked at the envelope in some surprise. He picked it up and opened it. He began to read.

'Oh, God,' he moaned.

'Bad news, son?' asked Sam.

Jon shook his head.

'I'm in the final,' he said.

'Jon!' cried Mary. 'How wonderful!'

She got up and threw her arms round his neck.

'Get off, Mother!' cried Jon, happily.

'How many others in it?' asked Sam.

'No other piano. The others will be clarinet, violin and that sort of thing.'

'You said there were a lot of entries for the piano. Older than you.'

'That's right.'

'And he's beaten them all!' beamed Mary.

'Obviously his age has done it. Being the youngest,' observed Sam.

'Not necessarily,' argued Mary.

'I'll have to practise more than ever now,' said Jon.

'Aren't you pleased with yourself?' asked Mary.

'Frightened,' admitted Jon.

'I can't wait to tell Louise,' declared Mary.

'And I must tell Pam,' said Jon.

'In the meantime,' put in Sam, 'I suggest you both eat your breakfast and keep your strength up.'

Once Sam had departed for the office there was a rush for the telephone. Mary won. Jon stood by impatiently while his mother chatted to her sister.

'Louise,' she exclaimed, 'what do you think? Jon's in the final for the Young Musician of the Year.'

'My!' cried Louise. 'Well done that boy!'

Then there followed a lot of waffle about the coming event, which this year evidently took place at a theatre in Covent Garden, and they would all be there cheering the boy on.

'I'm so excited,' confessed Mary.

She handed the telephone to Jon.

'Your aunt wants to speak to you.'

Jon took the telephone.

'Hello, Auntie.'

'Congratulations, darling.'

'Thank you. But I haven't won yet.'

'Never mind. There's someone here who wants to say something.'

Jon heard his cousin Pam saying, 'Well done, Maestro. We'll see you in the Albert Hall yet.'

'I hope you'll be coming to the event.'

'You bet. Me and Mother will be there rooting for you, darling.'

'Good. Mother and Dad will be there, of course.'

'That makes four of us to cheer you on.'

'I wonder who the judges will be.'

'Forget them. Just play.'

'I will.'

'See you.'

'See you.'

To Jon it was not a satisfactory conversation. He couldn't say what he really wanted to say because his mother was standing there, nor could Pam for the same reason. Instead of going to the piano to practise, as Mary thought he would, Jon went upstairs to his room. He wanted to talk to Jenni.

'Are you there, Jenni?' he asked.

'Yes, Jon. I'm here.'

'I'm worried about this competition.'

'Of course you are.'

'I was all agog to start with. Now I'm wondering if I haven't bitten off more than I can chew.'

'Music is your life, Jon. You might as well face it.'

'But what if I fail and have to go back to school?'

'Then you go back to school. It's only for this term.'

'What does the future hold?'

'I can't predict anything, Jon. I can only help you and encourage you. I can't put your fingers on the keys. All I can say is play as you normally do. Don't try to impress. Just go on and do it your way.'

'That's all I know.'

'That's all that's necessary.'

'I see.'

'Just keep practising.'

'I will.'

As Jon went downstairs to the front room he realised that he could never let Pam know about Jenni. Much as he would like to share everything with her and much as she might understand and be sympathetic, it was something he wanted to keep to himself. He even regretted ever telling his mother and father of the person he called his Guardian Angel. He was quite sure, though, that they had decided that his so-called obsession was over. As Jon's practice intensified, Sam began to complain of the sameness of the music.

'It's not something you can hum, for God's sake, is it?' he moaned to Mary.

'Neither is a lot of good music, dear.'

'That's why I don't like it.'

'You like his second piece, the Liszt.'

'Well, yes. That's not so bad.'

'You know, I still can't believe that our boy is the only

78

one chosen for the piano out of all those others. There's only one piano, you see. The rest are made up of clarinet, violin, and so on. But only one piano. And that's our Jon.'

'Yes, I know.'

'Aren't you proud of him?'

'It's not a question of pride. He's done well, I admit. But I'm thinking of his future.'

'So am I.'

'You think he's got a future in music?'

'Of course I do.'

'I wish I could share your faith.'

'It's not faith. It's his playing. He's got something.'

As an after-thought Mary suddenly said, 'I've just realised.'

'What?'

'He'll have to hire a dress suit.'

'Oh, Lord. Will he?'

'Well, of course.'

'I expect there's a hire place in the town.'

'I'll look in the Yellow Pages.'

'He won't need tails, will he? That means shirt and all that sort of thing.'

'No. I daresay dinner jacket will do.'

Louise rang to say that she had booked a table at the Savoy and Mary and Sam were invited to celebrate Jon's success or otherwise.

'Trust her,' commented Sam

'I think it's very kind of her,' protested Mary.

So the time came when Jon was to wear his first dinner jacket, and Mary decided that he looked very handsome. They took the car to the theatre and Sam managed to park. Mary and Sam made their way to the auditorium, while Jon proceeded to the stage door, where he was allocated a dressing room and shown the Green Room, where the contestants would gather. Mary and Sam sat next to Louise and Pam and there was great excitement amongst them, except for Sam, who was peculiarly monosyllabic. There were five contestants apart from Jon – violin, clarinet, French horn, harp and flute. The piano was allocated the last position, so poor Sam had to sit through hours of what he considered excruciating agony listening to noises he couldn't understand.

In the Green Room Jon did not mingle with the other contestants. He stood apart from them as they obviously knew each other from previous encounters at competitions. Jon gathered that much from their conversation.

Jon's relations in the audience were fearful of discussing the possibilities of the results in case they were overheard by their neighbours. The eager chatter of the packed theatre was quite deafening until the three judges, two men and one woman, eased their way into a specially segregated row in the Dress Circle. Then the audience became quiet as they realised that the show was about to start.

The Chairman of the event walked onto the stage and explained what was about to happen, which was what everybody present knew, of course. He then announced the first contestant, who was a young girl playing the clarinet accompanied by a gentleman at the piano. She was an attractive young girl who made the usual swoops and swirls as she played. The Stern family listened dutifully and applauded when everyone else did. The same applied when all the other young entrants performed. And then came Jon's turn. The family tensed themselves and looked up alertly. Jon walked onto the stage and stood in the front and bowed to the audience. He sat at the piano and ran his hands silently over the keys.

'What's he doing?' whispered Sam.

'Ssh!' breathed Mary.

Jon came out of his reverie, lifted his hands in the air and broke into Liszt's *Campanila*, which he played brilliantly as it was intended, with its intricate and difficult fingering. He did not look up from the keyboard throughout the piece. At the end there was enthusiastic applause with the family trying to outdo the others. The music that Jon had just played was recognised by Sam as 'that bloody thing' he used to complain about at home, but he realised what a difficult piece it was when he saw Jon's hands flying up and down the piano.

Jon did not acknowledge the applause but sat at the keyboard waiting to play something else. Once the audience had settled down, he looked up at some point in the air above the piano and began to play very quietly and casually the Liszt *Consolation No. 3*. This gentle, sentimental melody, enhanced Jon's expressive phrasing, floated round the auditorium. It had such an effect on the audience that, like Jon himself, they were almost afraid to breathe. It was only when Jon came to the descending chromatics near the end of the piece that he looked down and seemed to caress the keys thoughtfully. He then let his hands fall at his sides and just sat there. The audience was silent for a few seconds and then there erupted a thunderous torrent of applause, foot stamping and cheering. Mary, Louise and Pam sat with tears running down their cheeks and even the phlegmatic Sam had a lump in his throat. Jon stood by the piano, bowed and walked off the stage.

After a fairly long interval and during the usual buzz of conversation the Chairman led the judges onto the stage, where they were seated on chairs on one side while the contestants were invited to sit on chairs on the other side. The Senior Judge came forward and explained that the results would be announced in reverse order. He made the usual spiel about the high quality of musicianship that they had experienced and then proceeded to announce the winner of the third prize. This was the young girl who played the clarinet. She left her chair and moved forward to receive her prize from the judge. There was plenty of applause for her. The audience obviously liked her personality. The second prize went to the young man who played the violin in such a masterly manner. He again was applauded.

'We've blown it,' whispered Sam.

'Shut up,' hissed Mary.

And then the winner was announced.

'Jon Stern.'

At once there were screams of excitement and such loud applause that Pam was jumping up and down in her seat. There could be no doubt that the decision was popular. Jon shook hands with the judge and took hold of the silver trophy and the cheque, a substantial money award. He bowed to the audience and resumed his seat, where he was congratulated by the other two winners.

The Chairman concluded the proceedings in the usual platitudinous manner, everyone left the stage and the family left the auditorium.

Louise had a car waiting at the stage door and they all got in and waited for Jon to join them. A crowd of young girls soon gathered at the stage door and Louise nudged her sister.

'Look at that,' she said. 'Fans.'

The contestants, who filed out in their own time, were not bothered by the fans but when Jon came out they surged forward with their autograph books held aloft. He signed as many as he could, and this would have gone on for a long time if Pam hadn't opened the car door and called out.

'Jon! Come on!'

Jon suddenly stopped signing, eased his way through the crush with exclamations of 'excuse me, excuse me,' and escaped into the back of the car.

At the Savoy Grill there was champagne, and the toast, of course, was 'to Jon'. Jon sat next to Pam and, as an after-thought, took a visiting card from his pocket and handed it to her.

'A man came into the dressing room and gave me this. He said give him a ring.'

Pam took the card and read it.

'My God!' she exclaimed. 'You know who this is?'

'No idea,' admitted Jon.

'He's only the most famous and successful agent in the business.'

'Really?' said Jon.

'If he takes you under his wing you're made.'

'What's that?' asked Sam.

Pam explained the influence and reputation of the man, Jacob Cohen. She told the company that in the music world he was as famous as the famous performers he had promoted, performers that even Sam had heard of.

'What did he say?' asked Mary.

'All he did was thrust the card at me and say "give me a ring, young man".'

'How rude,' said Mary.

'Don't say that, dear,' warned Louise, 'if he can do the boy some good. You never know, there might be a contract in it.'

'Jon's not old enough to sign a contract,' said Sam.

'You can sign for him,' suggested Mary.

'If necessary, yes,' conceded Sam, evidently still doubtful of such a probability.

'You're going to have to put up with a lot of publicity, Jon,' warned Pam.

'Why?' he asked.

'Well, for one thing your youth, and the fact that you live at home and you're not sponsored by some music academy, like the others.'

'How do you know they were?'

'It was in the brochure.'

'If they want me,' declared Jon, 'they can see me at home. I'm not going to any studios or that sort of thing.'

After all the champagne and adulation, Sam realised that his car was parked near the theatre, so Louise's hire car was deported to drop off the Stern family before she and Pam could return home.

'Give me a ring, Jon,' urged Pam.

'I will,' he replied.

'And don't forget to ring that man.'

'I won't.'

Jon fell asleep on the way home. Mary wished that she could but she was too excited. Sam drove carefully and thoughtfully. At home that night he complained about Mary tossing and turning in bed.

'Can't you sleep?' he asked, irritably.

'No. I'm too worked up,' Mary complained.

'It could all be a flash in the pan, you know.'

'Oh, no! That agent man wants to talk to him. Pam says he's important.'

'What does Pam know?'

'She's up in these things. Being in London, too.'

'You ask an agent to sell your house. He doesn't always do it.'

'He's famous.'

'As an agent.'

'He could get Jon work.'

'He's got another term at school yet.'

'You can't hold him to that.'

'I can.'

'You wouldn't stand in the way, surely.'

'In the way of what?'

'If this agent man gets him work.'

'Depends on the work.'

Mary got out of bed hurriedly.

'If you stand in that boy's way I'll leave you!' she exclaimed.

'Oh, don't be an idiot,' cried Sam. 'Come back to bed. Let's wait and see what happens.'

Reluctantly Mary got back into bed.

One of the fascinating aspects of the inevitable photo-call, from the media point of view, was Jon's insistence on being photographed and interviewed in his modest suburban home, often with his mother and father. At one particularly trying photo session in the evening when he sat with his mother and father, he thought it would never end. The cameras kept flashing and the reporters kept asking questions. He stood up.

'That's enough. Sorry.'

He went out of the front room and found his way upstairs to his own room, leaving Sam and Mary to explain his absence, which they obviously put down to exhaustion. He shut the door and flopped down on his bed.

'Oh dear, Jenni,' he sighed. 'Sometimes I wish I'd never started this.'

'You've started it, you've got to go on,' said Jenni.

'I know. Thanks to you.'

'You did it, Jon. I didn't.'

'You helped. I always think of you helping when I'm playing.'

'You're going to be busy from now on.'

'I hope so.'

'You'll be famous.'

'I thought you didn't prophesy.'

'I'm not. You won't be able to help it once it gets going.'

'I must ring that man.'

'Yes. He's important.'

True to his promise, Jon telephoned Mr Cohen the next morning. The girl in reception said she couldn't put Mr Cohen through just like that. What did Jon want?

'He gave me his card last night after the show,' explained Jon.

'What show was that?'

'Young Musician of the Year. '

'Ah, yes. That. I knew he was there.'

'He asked me to ring him and that's what I'm doing. Or trying to.'

'What was your name again?'

'Jon Stern.'

'Oh, yes. You were the winner, weren't you?'

'That's right.'

'Hold the line.'

Jon waited patiently. Perhaps the girl was new, he decided. Then he heard the slightly rasping voice of Mr Cohen.

'Mr Stern! Thank you for ringing.'

'You asked me to.'

'Yes, I did. I'd like to talk to you, Mr Stern.'

'What about?'

'Why, your future, of course.'

'Oh, yes.'

'Where are you at the moment?'

'Home.'

'Where's that?'

'32 Oakley Road, Elmbury.'

'Can you come up to London?'

'Oh, yes.'

'I'd like to take you to lunch and we can talk.'

'When would you like?'

'What about tomorrow?'

'Yes. I can come tomorrow.'

'Good. Come to the office here at what, say, eleven thirty, and we can go on from there.'

'Thank you. I'll be there.'

'Look forward to seeing you.'

'Thank you.'

Jon put the phone down and called out to his mother, who was upstairs.

'Mother.'

'Yes?'

'I have to go to London tomorrow.'

Mary came downstairs to meet Jon in the hall by the telephone.

'Why? What's on?'

'Mr Cohen wants to see me. He wants to take me to lunch.'

'That's the agent man, isn't it?'

'Yes.'

'He might give you a job.'

'Let's hope so.'

As Mary returned to her chores upstairs Jon said, 'I'll give Pam a ring and tell her.'

He picked up the phone and dialled the number.

'Pam?'

'Oh, hello, Maestro. How's the genius this morning?'

'Come off it, Pam.'

'I'm still quivering with excitement.'

'I'm more worried than excited.'

'Why?'

'I've got to live up to it all now.'

'That shouldn't be difficult.'

'I'm coming up to London to see Mr Cohen tomorrow.'

'Oh, good. He'll point you in the right direction.'

'He's taking me to lunch.'

'That's an honour.'

'Is it?'

'Oh, yes. When you've seen him, why don't you come round and have tea and tell me all about it.'

'May I? I'd like that.'

'Of course. I'll look forward to it. I'll tell Mother.'

'Thanks, Pam. See you.'

'See you, Jon.'

Jon was almost as excited to be seeing Pam again as he was to be meeting Mr Cohen.

When Sam was told about the trip to London, he warned, 'Don't let him talk you into anything.'

'He can't, can he?' Jon reminded his father. 'I can't sign anything.'

'That's right.'

Mr Cohen's office was massive. The whole building was massive, a converted mansion in Park Lane. Wide stone steps led up to a portico with pillars either side of a double front door in glass and wrought iron. A brass plate at the side door told Jon that Jacob Cohen was on the first floor. Jon pushed open the heavy door and entered a marble-floored hall. There was a wide curving staircase on the left hand side and Jon began to climb it. There was no lift. He was aware once again of the quiet inside London houses considering the rush of buses and traffic outside in busy Park Lane. On the first landing he was confronted once again by an array of polished mahogany doors, one of which, in gilt lettering, displayed the name 'Jacob Cohen Enterprises'. He opened the door and went in. He found himself in a plush ante room. On one side of the room was an attractive secretary sitting at a Louis Quinze style desk. On the other side was a girl sitting at what looked like a mini telephone exchange. She was obviously the one who was so awkward on the phone to him. At the moment she was speaking in a foreign language he didn't recognise.

'Can I help you?' asked the secretary.

'I have an appointment with Mr Cohen.'

'Mr Stern, isn't it?'

'That's right.'

'I recognised you from the telly.'

She pressed a button on her desk and spoke into a machine.

'Mr Stern is here, sir,' she announced.

As she put the instrument down she got up from her desk.

'He'll see you now,' she said, leading the way to Mr Cohen's office. She opened the door and called, 'Mr Stern.'

Mr Cohen's office was sumptuous. Jon was conscious of gilt and ormolu, polished surfaces and a thick pile carpet of some dark red and dark blue mixture. Gilt-framed photographs on the wall depicted famous musicians and singers whom Jon recognised. He was very impressed.

'Mr Stern!' greeted Mr Cohen, effusively.

'Hello, Mr Cohen,' replied Jon, shaking the proffered hand.

'Sit down.'

As John sat on the gilded armchair Mr Cohen said, 'Congratulations again, young man.'

'Thank you.'

'A fantastic reception. I've never known anything like it. Even Peter Donahue in Moscow never got that much and his was fantastic, with people hanging out of windows calling to him.

'I was lucky', said Jon.

'No. It's not luck. It's style, attitude. That's what the audience liked. I know a lot of purists who would find fault with your playing but the public and the judges liked it. Style, that's the secret.'

'I still think I was lucky.'

'You can call it that. I call it style. So let's see what other people think. I take it you are prepared for me to represent you in the concert world?'

'Well, yes. I suppose so. I can't sign a contract, though.'

'Of course not. You're underage. But your father will do that for you, won't he?'

'I expect so. I'm supposed to be going back to school for another term but I'm not going.'

'Good. Now I suggest we start in a small way. The Wigmore Hall, for instance. It's a five-hundred-seater and it will get the critics used to you. What do you say?'

'I'm in your hands, Mr Cohen.'

'Not enormous financially but a start. Ideal for the kind of recital I envisage. You'll decide what you want to play. I wouldn't be surprised if that Liszt *Consolation* of yours becomes what you might call your signature tune. In a way that Solomon was always associated with the "Moonlight" Sonata.'

'I didn't know that.'

'Before your time but still in recent times. He was the first to emphasise that first movement adagio in its true sense, savouring every note.'

'That's what I like.'

90

'I noticed.'

Mr Cohen took Jon to lunch at the Dorchester Hotel. They walked down Park Lane. During the lunch Jon enjoyed what he called the good life. He only drank one glass of wine, which he wasn't all that keen on. At the end of the meal Mr Cohen said he would be sending Jon a contract for his father to sign and they shook hands and parted. Mr Cohen walked back up Park Lane while Jon made his way, by means of asking one or two people for directions now and then, to Aunt Louise's apartment. Pam opened the door to him.

'Hello, Maestro. Come in.'

As Jon entered the hall he asked, 'Where's Auntie?'

'Resting till tea time.'

'Oh.'

'Come in here.'

Pam took Jon by the hand and led him into the drawing room. He thought they were going to play duets.

'Now, sit down,' she commanded, 'and tell me all about your meeting with Jacob Cohen.'

They sat together on the sofa and Jon at once started on his recital, how he found the building in Park Lane, what the offices were like, how they walked down Park Lane to the Dorchester Hotel, how they had lunch in the Grill Room, how he drank a glass of wine.

'Not your first,' prompted Pam. 'You had champagne with us at the Savoy.'

'I know. I preferred it to the red wine we had at lunch.'

'That's right, dear. Start as you mean to go on.'

'Anyway, he's sending me a contract.'

'What for?'

'For him to be my agent and fix recitals.'

'Well, that can't hurt. He's very good. He should get you a lot of work.'

'He's suggesting the Wigmore Hall first off.'

'That piddling place.' Then she suddenly changed her mind. 'No. It's not a piddling place.'

'He said it was a good showcase.'

'That's true. It is. I would have wished for a larger hall. To show you off, dear.'

'Mr Cohen says critics are often put off by the audience if they're too enthusiastic. They go the other way.'

'In other words, the Wigmore Hall will be for the critics with a certain amount of audience thrown in.'

'Something like that.'

'Clever thinking. Incidentally, I've got a book of Bartok duets. We'll try them in a minute, but first...'

She took Jon's face in her hands and gave him an open-mouthed kiss, touching his tongue with hers. She threw her leg across his so that he could more easily put his hand up her skirt. Neither needed further invitation.

They were disturbed by the sound of Aunt Louise moving about in the corridor. As they straightened their clothing Pam said, 'Have a look at the Bartok.'

'I will.'

He went over to the piano, took the album from the desk and turned the pages.

'Shall we try it?' he asked.

'I've tried the secondo, if you'll take the primo.'

'Let's see.'

They sat together on the long piano stool.

'Ready?' asked Jon.

'On three. Three, two, one.'

Aunt Louise heard the music as she came along the corridor and was glad to know that the cousins were together enjoying themselves. She decided, for that reason, to avoid the drawing room and went directly to the kitchen to prepare the tea. She thought she would put the tea and cakes on a trolley and wheel it into the drawing room for the cousins.

Pam and Jon were coming to the end of the Bartok when the sound was augmented by the rattle of tea cups as Aunt Louise wheeled in the trolley. At once Jon got up from the piano and embraced his aunt.

'Hello, Aunt!' he enthused.

'Hello, Maestro,' greeted Aunt Louise.

'You, too,' remarked Jon.

'Me too what?' asked Louise.

'That's what Pam called me when I got here.'

'Well, that's what you are.'

'Oh, good. Tea,' exclaimed Pam.

Louise poured the tea from the trolley while Pam handed round the cakes.

'You've seen Mr Cohen, I believe, Jon,' said Louise.

'Yes. He's fixing up for me to play at the Wigmore Hall. But Dad has to sign the contract.'

'Let's hope he does,' commented Louise.

'Surely he wouldn't stand in the way,' declared Pam.

'You never know with him. First thing he'll do is query Mr Cohen's fee, I bet you. Always the accountant.'

'Oh, he's not as bad as that,' asserted Jon.

'He was always a misery,' persisted Louise. 'I always told my sister so.'

'They've been very happy all these years,' insisted Jon.

'Amazing,' Louise went on. 'But then Mary never approved of my own husband. She always said he was too sharp, whatever that meant. He certainly did well for himself. And us. Which is more than Sam can say.'

'I don't think Jon's interested in family squabbles, Mother,' advised Pam.

'They're not squabbles,' corrected Louise. 'Just sisterly differences.'

'I'd better begin to make my way to the station,' said Jon.

'I'll walk with you,' suggested Pam.

'Oh. That's kind of you.'

'When you're doing the Wigmore Hall, Jon,' declared Louise, 'you'll stay here, won't you? You don't want to go up and down each day.'

'I'll have to ask Mother,' said Jon.

'Do that. I'll give her a ring, anyway.'

'Thank you.'

Jon kissed his aunt on the cheek dutifully and, accompanied by Pam, left the apartment. Louise watched them go. She now always thought of them as 'those two'. It seemed so natural.

She needn't have worried about Sam's attitude to the contract. He was delighted to sign it and send it off straight away, at the same time congratulating his son.

'We're on our way,' declared Mary, delightedly.

'Ssh!' warned Sam. 'Don't count your chickens.'

'I don't care about the chickens,' said Jon, who was sitting with them at breakfast. 'It's the eggs I want to see.'

'Talking of eggs,' put in Sam, 'you know you've got another term at school, Jon.'

'Oh, no!' moaned Mary.

'That is,' Sam went on with a smile, 'if you can spare the time from your concerts.'

'Thanks, Dad.'

'I'll have to write to the Headmaster.'

And so it was left. After the heartaches and arguments of the past it was now understood that Jon could pursue his musical career.

The publicity announcing Jon Stern's first public

appearance since winning the Young Musician of the Year competition included fly posters showing his portrait at various vantage points across London, including underground stations and buses, much to the amusement of Pam and Sam. Sam's colleagues were not slow to rib him about it, which flattered him. His whole attitude to his son's ambition had changed and he was enjoying the reflected glory.

Mr Cohen invited all the music critics and booking agents for such prestigious establishments as the Albert Hall, the Festival Hall and the Barbican, together with those involved in booking continental tours and venues in America. It didn't leave much room for the general public but as Jon was playing at the Wigmore Hall for the whole week they had plenty of chance to hear him if they wanted to.

The family, of course, attended the first night and went away somewhat disappointed. They had expected Jon to receive a standing ovation as had been the custom, but at the end of his recital it was only the family and friends who applauded with anything like enthusiasm. The recital was appreciated, of course, but no-one expected the critics or the booking agents to show too much approval. It would be contrary to their interests. Jon tried to explain to his father that this audience was mostly made up of non-paying critics and agents. The rest, he suggested, would come during the week.

The critics wrote favourable reviews of the event, which was some consolation. They criticised the content of the programme – Rachmaninoff, Scriabin, Balakirev – for being predominantly Russian, though they praised Jon's own favourite, the Liszt *Consolation*. They praised Jon's style of playing, suggesting that his treatment of the music gave it an air of newness which they found refreshing.

For the rest of the week the Wigmore Hall was sold out, and although Pam was the only member of the family to attend every night, she gave her mother, Mary and Sam to understand that every night there was a standing ovation with demands for encores. Although Jon was staying at his aunt's apartment for the duration of the booking, he, too, phoned home with the news.

'It looks as if we've got a famous son on our hands,' said Mary, as they were preparing for bed.

'Beats me where he gets it from,' confessed Sam. 'Mind you, he says music is mathematics, so perhaps my accountancy…'

'Don't kid yourself dear,' scoffed Mary. 'I was a pianist, remember.'

'I know you were.'

'I passed all my exams.'

'So you told me.'

'I could have gone on with it.'

'Only for yourself.'

'What do you mean?'

'Playing for yourself and friends. The drawing room sing-song, not concert work. This boy looks like being famous. I would never have believed it.'

'Fathers doubt. It's mothers who believe in their children.'

'Oh, you mothers are wonderful, aren't you?'

'We are. You couldn't do what we do.'

'What's that?'

'Have genius children.'

'We won't go into that. I don't know what you'd have done if I hadn't been there.'

'That is being worked on by some scientist, I believe.'

Sam could not reply because he had fallen asleep.

Pam and Jon were also asleep in the same bed, as had become their habit. They hated being parted when the time came for Jon to relinquish his tenure at the Wigmore Hall. He had to return to his own home to the accompaniment of Pam's tears.

Fortunately for them, the interval before engagements was not very long. Mr Cohen did not find it difficult to find Jon work. He was very much in demand for two reasons. One was the novelty of the boy, his acclaim as Young Musician of the Year and his television appearance on that programme. The other was his unique musicianship. Something had captivated his audiences in spite of the familiarity of the music.

The next engagement was at the Barbican, again in London, prompting Sam to ask Mary if they shouldn't contribute something to Aunt Louise's board and lodging as it seemed to be taken for granted that any London engagement entailed Jon's lodging there.

'I've often suggested it,' explained Mary. 'But Louise won't hear of it.'

'Well, we can only offer, I suppose,' conceded Sam.

'In any case,' Mary went on, 'I believe he and Pam are getting on rather well.'

'Oh. She's another one, isn't she?'

'Another what?'

'Music mad.'

'Yes. Evidently they play duets together.'

'Oh, dear. It's all happening, isn't it?'

'Aren't you pleased?'

'Relieved.'

'Because he's earning?'

'Well, naturally. My only worry is how long will it last?'

'As long as he plays as he does.'

'It's not just because he's young and good-looking?'

'No. I wouldn't think so. There are plenty of successful pianists who are far from good-looking.'

'I hope you're right. I'll get him to put something

aside for a rainy day. I could recommend some good investments.'

'His best investments are his own fingers.'

The Barbican engagement was so successful that Mr Cohen was able to book him at the Festival Hall. Pam attended all his appearances and they stayed together overnight.

The most excitement for the family was the engagement at the Royal Albert Hall. It was a booking for one night only and for that reason, no doubt, the box office was a complete sell-out. Sam was so elated that he took a box for his family and friends, with champagne laid on in the room at the back. Among his friends were one or two of his colleagues at the office and their wives. On this occasion it wasn't necessary for Jon to stay overnight with Pam. Sam drove him home in the family car. Mr Cohen declared that the scenes at the Albert Hall had never been equalled and the owners wanted to repeat the engagement, but Mr Cohen, in his wisdom, refused that. For the moment he was satisfied with the one-night stand, there would be time at a later date for a reprise in the prestigious Albert Hall. He was expounding on these ideas to the family in the box during the interval. He told them that he was planning a promised tour for Jon that would take in such places as Bournemouth, Cardiff, Birmingham, Edinburgh and so on.

'The poor boy will be worn out,' complained Mary.

'Oh, no, Mrs Stern,' assured Mr Cohen. 'I'll see that doesn't happen.'

'Will he be on his own?' persisted Mary.

'On his own?'

'Yes,' explained Mary. 'He'll want someone to keep him company, make sure his room is comfortable and so on. Make sure he eats properly.'

'Well, of course,' conceded Mr Cohen. 'I have an

agent in each location, but he's not a nanny, I'm afraid.'

'I'm not talking about a nanny,' insisted Mary. 'I'm talking about common or garden companionship, which I would have thought necessary for his work.'

'I could go with him,' put in Pam eagerly. 'I could be his companion-minder.'

'That's an idea,' cried Louise.

'I can make sure his room's comfortable and make sure he eats properly,' explained Pam

'I'd be happy with that,' confessed Mary.

Poor Mr Cohen was not used to such an inquisition about his artistes but, then again, Jon Stern was quite the youngest artiste that he had ever had to deal with. Admittedly he was quite unsophisticated and hardly a man of the world, but if the girl was to accompany him it would mean an extra room at each hotel. A pity they couldn't share a room, he thought cynically. Little did he know that Pam would be spending the nights in Jon's bedroom suite and that her own room would be used simply as a bathroom, with the bed discreetly disarranged to confuse the chambermaids.

Consequently, what started as a sentimental interlude became a passionate and serious involvement for the two of them and during the provincial tour they even spoke of marriage. At such moments all thoughts of Jenni were forgotten and Jon behaved as though she had never existed. Yet when he played the piano, no matter where or when, his thoughts immediately turned to her, resulting in what people called his style.

The gossip writers and media hounds were not slow to notice the affinity that appeared to exist between Jon and Pam and very soon dubbed them the Cosi Cousins, borrowing from Mozart's *Cosi fan tutti*. Jon and Pam enjoyed the joke but it caused Mary some concern. She was aware of the friendly relationship between her son and his cousin but she had no idea that it was more than that. She telephoned her sister.

'Louise,' she cried. 'What's going on?'

'Going on?' asked Louise. 'Where?'

'With Jon and Pam.'

'Why? What's the problem?'

'It says in the paper they're having an affair.'

'No, it doesn't.'

'I've just read it.'

'So have I '

'Well?'

'It simply suggests that they're close. As they are.'

'How close?'

'I don't know how close. What are you worried about?'

'Well, it looks as if they're … well … you know … sort of…'

'Would that matter?'

'No. Not really. I didn't mean that. I'd just like to know.'

'My dear, you know as much as I do. They get on very well together. They play duets together. What else they do together I've no idea.'

'So long as that's all it is.'

'Mary! Don't be such a prude. Or are you suggesting that my Pam isn't good enough for your Jon now that he's making a name for himself?'

'No. No. Nothing like that. It's just that…'

'A bit of romance wouldn't do Jon any harm.'

'So long as it doesn't affect his career.'

'I don't know if you've noticed, dear, but Pam is actually helping him in his career. That's why she's with him on tour at the moment.'

'She's with him, I know.'

'Keeping him company, looking after him, talking to him, listening to him. She's as interested in music as he is and I think they make a nice couple.'

'Do you?'

'Don't you?'

'Of course, yes. Oh, I don't know what to think.'

'I suggest we both leave them alone to sort themselves out.'

'If you say so…'

And that was the end of the conversation. The two sisters very rarely argued with each other. They never actually quarrelled but the veiled difference was always there. Mary, for her part, wished for someone famous or socially elevated for Jon's wife now that he was becoming famous himself. Louise, on the other hand, was concerned that if marriage was being considered, then Pam was the ideal wife for Jon – if only because they knew each other so well. As for physical attributes, Pam had a splendid figure, as several young men had noticed before now and she was sure that Jon was not blind.

As far as Jon and Pam were concerned, they found that the bed was the answer to any pent-up anxieties or nerves that accompanied each recital as they proceeded on their tour. At the end of the tour, exhausting as it was, the two of them decided to go away for a holiday.

'Jon and I are going away for a holiday. He needs it,' Pam told her mother.

'Don't you?'

'Of course.'

'Where are you going?'

'South of France. Get some sunshine.'

'Will you fly?'

'No. Jon wants to drive.'

'Has he told his mother?'

'I don't know.'

'I'll be interested to know her reaction.'

'You don't mind, do you?'

'Good Heavens, no. But I'm not Mary.'

'She won't object, surely.'

'She might not, but *he* might.'

'Uncle Sam?'

'Yes. Jon can't exactly please himself.'

'But in this day and age … I can't believe that any parent could be so stuffy.'

'You don't know your Uncle Sam.'

'Are you serious?'

'Quite.'

'I can't wait for Jon to ring.'

Actually, Jon was quite direct with his mother.

'I need a holiday,' he said. 'The tour was exhausting.'

'Oh, I don't think your father can get away just yet,' demurred Mary.

'I was going on my own.'

'Oh. Very well.'

She could hardly conceal her disappointment. She had imagined that the three of them could go away together, as they'd always done. She had forgotten for the moment that Jon now lived in a world of his own.

'Where will you go?' she asked, without enthusiasm.

'I thought the South of France.'

'Oh, we've never been there.'

'I could do with some sun.'

'Couldn't we all! I wonder how much the fare is.'

'I'll drive.'

'Drive? You don't know the way.'

'I can find it. I'll get a route. I'll take Pam with me. She can navigate.'

'Pam?'

'Yes. Why not?'

'What about hotels?'

'What about them?'

'Will you be staying in the same hotels?'

'Of course. In the same towns, too.'

'In separate rooms, I hope.'

'Naturally.'

'That's alright then.'

'Grow up, Mother. Please.'

'I'm thinking of your father. You know what he's like with all his cronies. He doesn't approve of the modern ways of going on. I'll have to break the news to him about Pam.'

'Tell him what you like, Mother. She's coming with me.'

'He may not approve.'

'Mother, I've been staying in hotels all over the country with Pam. What's the difference?'

'That was work. This is France. Softly, softly, dear.'

'I get it.'

With that he left his mother and went to his room upstairs, where Jenni spoke to him.

'You're growing up fast, Jon,' she said.

'Jenni!' exclaimed Jon, happily. 'Where have you been?'

'Watching.'

'That was some tour, wasn't it?'

'Wonderful. There's more to come.'

'Oh, I hope so.'

'You've been too busy for us to talk.'

'I've thought of you.'

'I know you have. But I'm glad that Pam is helping you.'

'You like her, don't you?'

'Oh, yes. She's very good for you.'

'You'll come to France with us, won't you?'

'Of course.'

'I wondered because it's a foreign country.'

'Oh, we have no boundaries.'

'That's good.'

'I won't leave you, Jon.'

'Thank you.'

That evening when Sam arrived home Mary could not wait to tell him about Jon and Pam wanting to go to France.

'Together?' asked Sam, in alarm.

'Yes.'

'That's a bit thick, isn't it?'

'That's what I thought at first.'

'On the tour was different.'

'That's what I said. That was work.'

'I suppose we can't stop them.'

'Well, hardly. He needs the rest.'

'He could rest here. Cornwall or somewhere.'

'He says he wants the sun.'

'Don't we all?'

'That's what I said.'

'It's something we've got to expect now, I reckon.'

'At least with Pam it's someone we know.'

'What does your sister say?'

'She doesn't seem to mind.'

'She wouldn't.'

There was a glum silence between the parents.

'It's a different world, isn't it?' mused Mary.

'What is?'

'His and ours.'

'Well, yes. He's a bit of a public figure now.'

'He doesn't seem to belong to us any more.'

'Who doesn't?' asked Jon, cheerily, as he came downstairs to join his parents in the sitting room.

'You, dear,' explained Mary.

'Going on your hols, Jon, I hear,' said Sam.

'That's right.'

'With a lady.'

'Yes. Pam. She's going to help with the driving.'

'That all?'

Jon ignored the insinuation.

'We'll see the sights together.'

'Separate rooms, I hope.'

'Of course,' lied Jon, for the second time.

'I don't hold with all this modern promiscuity.'

'Neither do I, Dad. If you like someone, then stay with them, I say.'

'How long will you be away, dear?' asked Mary.

'From what I can make out,' replied Jon, 'it takes two or three days to get down there. Depending on what sight-seeing you do. Then a week there, three days back, I'd say a fortnight or so.'

'I envy you,' said Sam.

'I'll treat you and Mother to the trip if you like,' offered Jon.

'What!' exclaimed Sam.

'Why not?' persisted Jon. 'I owe you that much.'

'No,' said Sam. 'We wouldn't hear of it. I'm just glad you're able to pay your own way.'

'Very kind of you to make the offer, dear,' said Mary.

'Perhaps when it comes round to my holiday period at the office...' suggested Sam.

'Why not?' agreed Jon. 'The offer still stands.'

Sam adopted a serious, magisterial manner.

'Jon,' he began, 'I know that you now live in a different world from ours and you'll no doubt be setting up your own place–'

'There'll always be a home for you here,' interrupted Mary.

'As I was saying,' continued Sam, glaring at Mary. 'I think you should always bear in mind that we're ordinary, simple people not used to gossip and scandal.'

'What on earth are you trying to say, Dad?' asked Jon.

'I'm trying to say, son, that I hope there's no shenanigans going on with you and Pam.'

There was a stunned silence in the room. Even Mary was somewhat disconcerted by her husband's remark. Jon looked his father straight in the eye.

'That's an insult to Pam.'

With that he turned on his heel and went into the front room, where he was soon playing the piano with some gusto, as if in a rage.

'He doesn't usually play like that,' remarked Sam.

'You've upset him.'

'Over Pam?'

'Well, of course.'

'I thought you said they were close.'

'So they are. That's why he resents your remark.'

'I can't win, can I?'

'I wouldn't try, dear. Just leave them alone.'

They expected the usual postcards from the two holidaymakers, which were gratefully received. What they didn't expect was a copy of a popular photo-magazine offered to them one evening by their neighbour, Mrs Hunt, showing candid pictures of Jon and Pam cavorting in the sun in the South of France. There were bosom and bottom shots of Pam in her brief bikini and shots of the two of them embracing amorously. There was a shot of Pam sitting in Jon's lap and the obligatory shot of the two of them, back view, walking along the beach arms round waists, Pam looking as if she had nothing on her lower half. Sam and

Mary were horrified to see such evidence of what looked like a torrid affair. Mrs Hunt was amused by their reaction.

'Didn't you know?' she asked.

'Know what?' Mary asked.

'They were together.'

'Oh, yes,' explained Mary. 'They told us they were going away.'

'Can we keep the magazine?' asked Sam.

'Oh, no,' declared Mrs Hunt. 'My daughter wants it for her scrapbook. She has every picture of Jon since he started.'

'I'll get one at the newsagent,' said Sam.

'Well, I thought you'd like to see it.'

'Yes, Mrs Hunt,' said Mary. 'Thank you for showing us.'

As she was leaving, Mrs Hunt said, 'Such is fame, Mrs Stern.'

Once the neighbour had gone back to her own house Mary went at once to phone her sister.

'Louise?'

'Oh, hello, Mary.'

'Have you seen those disgusting pictures of Jon and Pam...?'

Before she could continue, Louise interrupted her.

'What's disgusting about them?'

'Why, Pam's practically naked.'

'That's nothing these days, dear. I thought they looked very happy.'

'Did you know the affair was going on?'

'I don't know about an affair. I knew they were friendly and I'm pleased for them.'

'That's all very well. You're in London. It's different here. What with the neighbours and the people in Sam's office. What are they to think?'

'Mary, stop being stupid. The two of them are very happy together and that's all that matters. They're not children, for God's sake.'

'I'm sorry you see it that way.'

'There's no other way.'

'I'm afraid there is.'

'Go to it, then, dear.'

'Goodbye, Louise.'

Without waiting for Louise to reply she put the phone down and returned to her husband.

'What does she say?' asked Sam.

'She seems to think nothing of it.'

'She wouldn't.'

'I don't blame her.'

'I do. He deceived us.'

'I'm not sure about Pam. I know she's a relative and all that, but we don't know much about her, do we?'

'We do now, looking at those pictures.'

'I always thought she was rather modern. That's living in London.'

'I call it promiscuous.'

'Oh, I wouldn't say that. She's not with just anybody. She's with Jon.'

'I'll have something to say to him when he gets back.'

'I think we should leave them alone.'

'You're changing your tune, aren't you?'

'Those pictures were a shock, I admit, but if he's happy…'

'Anyone would be happy cavorting about like that. It's not very dignified. God knows what my chairman will think. He came to the Albert Hall.'

'And he'll come again, I expect.'

'This could put him off.'

'As Mrs Hunt just said, that's fame.'

'Huh?'

Mary could see visions of Jon and Pam married, Jon leaving home and a whole new world that would take him away from her. She was both happy and sad about that; happy for him, sad for herself having to give him up.

Jon and Pam themselves were unaware that their pictures were appearing in the magazine until they crossed the Channel and Pam bought it at the bookstall. They had been driving across country and were that much out of touch. She showed the pictures to Jon and they both laughed out loud.

'Just look at you!' exclaimed Jon.

'I wonder who took them?' mused Pam.

'Some enterprising camera freak who sold them to the magazine.'

'I didn't notice anybody, did you?'

'No.' Then as an afterthought Jon said, 'Poor Dad. He'll be drummed out of the Brownies.'

'My mother won't worry,' declared Pam.

Sam Stern, as expected, had his leg pulled unmercifully when he appeared in the office. All his colleagues had seen the pictures.

'Lovely boobs,' said one.

'Nice bum,' said another.

'I wish I'd kept up my piano lessons,' said another.

Sam took it all in good part, though he hated it and was not slow to complain to his wife when he got home.

'That boy is becoming an embarrassment,' he declared.

'We'll have to get used to it.'

'I can't get used to a way of life that is complete anathema to me.'

'You must remember that he's an artist and artists have different ideas of what is right and what is wrong.'

'He knew what was right and wrong before he became an artist. There's another thing that puzzles me.'

'What's that?'

'He doesn't seem to want to leave home. Usually kids like him can't wait to set up on their own.'

'I'm grateful for that,' said Mary.

'Oh, I know. You'd want to hold on to him because you're a mother.'

'It's not only that. He seems to like it here, away from hotels and people. I don't think he likes London all that much. Besides, if he had a place of his own, who would look after him?'

'Pam, I expect.'

'You mean live together?'

'People do today, don't they?'

'I don't think even Louise would approve of that.'

'You surprise me.'

'Oh, come on. Louise's not like that.'

'She's not like us. I give you that.'

'I don't like you talking like that about my sister.'

The silence that followed developed into a quiet and peaceful evening watching television.

Mr Cohen had not been idle in the meantime. He had been busy organising an extensive and highly remunerative tour of America. He told Jon, as the boy sat in his office, that the tour was something of an accolade, embracing, as it did, the whole country. Again Jon insisted on his cousin accompanying him as his personal assistant.

'No problem,' agreed Mr Cohen.

'I think she should be paid this time,' said Jon.

'Paid?' echoed Mr Cohen, horrified.

'On the last tour she came as a volunteer and I put

110

her up at my hotels, but in America I would expect her accommodation to be paid for plus a salary.'

'If you think you need a personal assistant then I think you should pay for her.'

'Oh, no.'

'The sponsors in America would expect it. They'd say you don't need an assistant because they have their own area managers, as you saw on your last tour.'

'Then we don't go.'

'Don't say that, Jon. They're very keen.'

'If they're keen they'll pay.'

'For your age, Jon, you're quite grown up when it comes to a bargain.'

'I'm not playing anywhere as a bargain. I play to please.'

'Of course. I'll get back to the sponsors. Let you know.'

'Thank you.'

As he was in the vicinity Jon decided to call on Pam, who was delighted to see him. He told her about the proposed American tour and that he had insisted on her travelling with him. She screamed with delight and ran to her mother, who was in the kitchen.

'Mother!'

'What on earth's the matter?' Louise asked.

'We're going to America!'

Jon had joined Pam in the kitchen, and Louise turned to him.

'Hello, Jon. What's my girl on about?'

'I've just been to see Mr Cohen and he's fixed up a tour of America. I'm insisting on Pam going with me.'

'Isn't that wonderful?' exclaimed Pam.

Louise was somewhat subdued.

'That sounds like a long tour,' she said.

'I expect it will be,' agreed Jon.

'I shall miss you both.'

'Oh, Mother! We'll be on the phone,' assured Pam.

Even at such an early stage in the venture Louise was inclined to be tearful.

'Tell you what,' declared Jon, 'why don't we all go down to the Dorchester and have lunch to celebrate.'

'Why not?' agreed Pam.

'Give me time to change,' said Louise.

Although Mr Cohen had not yet confirmed the appointment of Pam on the tour, Jon felt convinced that it would be approved. If it wasn't he would organise it himself, something he would not admit to Mr Cohen.

After an enjoyable lunch at the Dorchester Hotel Jon made his way home, where his mother greeted him with the news:

'I didn't know you were going to America, Jon.'

'Neither did I until I saw Mr Cohen this morning.'

'He rang while you were out. He gave me a message for you. Pam's salary has been agreed.'

'Oh, good.'

'So you're off with her again?'

'As we did on the last tour, yes.'

'Getting quite a thing, isn't it?'

'What is?'

'You and Pam.'

'It works very well.'

'I'm sure it does.'

'Don't be sarcastic, Mother. It doesn't suit you.'

'You're certainly seeing the world, dear.'

'There's a lot of it left: Europe, Australia, Japan.'

'I expect Mr Cohen will be fixing you up with all those in time.'

'I hope so.'

'I'm proud of you, Jon.'

'Thank you, Mother. Jenni certainly started something, didn't she?'

'Jenni?'

Mary was shocked to hear the name that she and Sam had decided was dead and buried.

'When she helped me with my homework.'

'Oh, that. Yes.'

'She got me through the Musician of the Year.'

'How? You have your own way of playing. That's your secret, as the critics have said. Jenni can't make you do that.'

'She whispers to me while I'm playing, "Slow down a bit. Softly now." That way I don't get stale, like some pianists who are so familiar with the music they just play it without thinking.'

'I didn't know that. Does that mean you couldn't play like that without her?'

'Oh, I wouldn't say that because I would always remember what she said.'

Mary was more than shocked by the revelation. To realise that Jenni still existed was bad enough, but her influence was frightening. It made Jon nothing but an automaton in spite of his unique style of playing. She was somewhat relieved when he went on to say, 'To tell the truth I don't know where she starts and where she stops. It's just nice to know she's there.'

'Does she know about Pam?'

'Oh, yes. She knows I'm fond of her.'

'How does she know that?'

'I told her.'

'You did?'

'Yes. We have no secrets from each other, me and Jenni. What would you like me to bring you back from New York?'

'Nothing, dear. Just yourself.'

'I'll look for something for Dad.'

'He'll like that.'

It was Jon's idea that the American tour should not start in New York but should end there. In that way, he considered, word of mouth, gossip – or whatever it was called – could trickle back to New York and so incite interest.

And that is, in fact, what happened. The tour was extensive and, according to Pam, not a little exhausting. John's recitals caused gossip and controversy wherever he performed, either because of his style of playing or his youthful, handsome appearance. Audiences were enthusiastic to the point of ecstasy and the critics accepted what they called the phenomenon. Jon was feted and lionised wherever he went and Pam was accepted as his partner. At supper parties Jon and Pam would sit at a piano and play together, not necessarily classical music, which was their stock-in-trade, but popular and even amusing pieces. It was a joke, and hugely enjoyable. It also made the gossip columns and America take them to its heart.

That is, with the exception of New York. Jon's plan to play first to what was known as 'the sticks' and then conclude in the famous city very nearly misfired. The New York press was upset that they should be the last in the line. There were grumblings and Pam was worried that they might have made a mistake.

'If it's a mistake, darling,' Jon soothed her, 'it's not anybody's fault but mine.'

'It would be a shame if after all the successes you've had so far it should fall down now. In New York of all places.'

They were sitting in Jon's suite in the Plaza Hotel.

114

Copies of newspapers were spread about the room, the contents of which led Pam to be fearful of their reception in the city. They were virtually saying who does this upstart think he is.

'It doesn't sound very hopeful, does it?' suggested Pam.

'It could have been the same the other way round,' explained Jon. 'The people in the sticks could be saying who does this New York chap think he is.'

'I suppose so, yes.'

'Anyway, let's forget the critics and go and play to our friends.'

'Yes. Let's.'

They diverted to their separate bedrooms to change their clothes for the concert. As they made their way to Jon's dressing room at the theatre, Pam said, 'I think I'll have a chair beside the stage tonight.'

'Oh, why?' asked Jon.

'I don't fancy sitting in the audience.'

'You usually do. You pick up bits of gossip.'

'I know. Not tonight. Not here.'

'You still worried about the press?'

'I just don't want to be near them in case.'

'Pity. I like to see you out there when I'm playing.'

'I'll sit facing you.'

'Good.'

Pam sat on a chair in the wings, facing the pianist. She saw Jon come onto the platform. The applause was polite rather than enthusiastic. She saw him rest his hand on the piano as he made his bow. She saw him flick back the tails of his coat as he sat on the stool. He sat for a few brief moments as if meditating. Then, to Pam's complete surprise and astonishment, he began to play a simple and beautiful piece of music called *To a Wild Rose,* which she knew was written by an American named

Edward Macdowall. Jon was obviously deviating from his usual programme. Pam wondered why. He followed that with his own version of Gershwin's *Walking the Dog*, which he made amusing by every now and then looking back and pausing to give the impression that the dog had stopped at a lamp post. The audience understood and chuckled. Pam was getting worried that he was turning a serious piano recital into a vaudeville act. But she needn't have worried. As soon as the laughter and applause had died down, he crashed into the Rachmaninoff prelude like a motor cycle smashing through a plate glass window, such was the shock to the audience. Now the recital was on, Pam decided. At the end of the prelude the applause was thunderous. Jon did not bow, neither did he wait for the applause to die down, but embarked immediately on the Liszt *Camponile*, which is quite histrionically showy. Pam was relieved when she realised how the audience was reacting, no matter what the critics might have to say. The audience were enjoying Jon's performance and when he got up from the piano to take his bow the enthusiasm was obvious. When Jon sat down again he waited before proceeding with his now famous finale, the Liszt *Consolation*. He sat playing with his head up as if asleep. There was actually a slight murmur in the audience as if in appreciation as he was playing. At the end there was silence. And then, as he stood up, there was such a burst of applause as if a dam had burst forth with a roar. It was more than a standing ovation, it was more like a stampede. Jon continued to bow with a warm smile. It was not his habit to play encores because he did not want to disturb the calm atmosphere created by the *Consolation*. For that reason the more the audience called for 'Encore', the more he shook his head.

Pam left her seat in the wings and hurried to Jon's

dressing room and when he came in they threw their arms round each other.

'Wonderful! Wonderful!' cried Pam.

They were invaded almost immediately by a horde of VIPs, television cameras and the press. The noise was deafening and the crush suffocating. A great deal of champagne was both drunk and wasted by people bumping into each other and spilling it. Jon met the critics amicably and not a word was said about the concert.

When at last Jon and Pam reached their apartment in the hotel, they were excited and exhausted. Jon went directly into the bedroom and fell on the bed.

'I don't care what they say,' he cried, 'I enjoyed myself.'

'So did I,' agreed Pam, falling on the bed beside him.

Fully dressed, they fell asleep. When they woke up, some time in the early morning, they undressed and got into bed together.

Later in the morning the sitting room was littered with newspapers and Jon and Pam were poring over them, scanning the reviews.

'"The pianist who knows how to please",' recited Pam.

'They've all picked on *The Wild Rose* and *Walking the Dog*. A sop to New Yorkers, they call it,' said Jon.

'Here's an interesting bit,' announced Pam. '"Jon Stern has a tentative way of playing the piano as if he is fearful of being heard. It is like a child's first attempt with added maturity. And then, to confuse us all, he will launch into the most difficult piano music that could be imagined with all the gusto at his command."'

'They've got this bit right,' quoted Jon, "Jon Stern is the only concert pianist who refuses to play an encore.

At the risk of offending his audience he considers that any encore would spoil the atmosphere created by the Liszt *Consolation*." I told him that and he's reported it.'

'If you did encores,' admitted Pam, 'we'd have been there all night.'

Jon tossed the newspapers aside.

'Better than I thought,' he declared. 'What about you?'

'A triumph, I'd say,' admitted Pam, as she left her chair and threw herself at Jon, and amid laughter and squeals, they eventually made love.

There were numerous newspaper interviews and television appearances before Jon had time to do some shopping for his family, and even then he was pursued by gentlemen with cameras. With Pam's help he was able to buy something for his mother and father, and Pam herself managed to buy something for her mother. Jon would have liked to buy something for Jenni but he realised that that was impossible. She would know, however, that the thought was there.

At last they were on the plane for home. What then, Jon wondered. What had Mr Cohen lined up for him? A tour of Europe? That's all that was left, it seemed. There were recording sessions, of course. He didn't enjoy doing those, although they sold very well, because of the tedium involved with the sound crews. There was always Australia, of course, but he would leave it to Mr Cohen.

At London Airport Jon and Pam went their separate ways, the goodbye kiss being recorded by some newsman's camera and appearing in the paper next morning. It was a happy photograph in spite of the occasion.

Jon arrived home to be met ecstatically by his mother and father, who were bowled over by their presents and wanted to hear all about the trip. Jon had collected the newspaper reviews especially for them and presented them with the whole bunch so that they read all about it at will. Jon had so much to tell them that he didn't know where to start and they were so pleased to have him back that they didn't ask a lot of questions.

'I hope you can stay with us for a little while now,' said Mary.

'So do I,' Jon told her.

'There's nothing like your own bed, Jon,' declared Sam.

'I'm looking forward to that,' admitted Jon.

And he actually was. When he went up to bed he called to Jenni, 'Hello, Jenni. I'm back.'

'I know. I was with you on the tour.'

'Of course you were. I always think of you as being in this room, though, because it's where I first met you.'

'I'm with you wherever you go.'

'Yes. I feel it. I'd miss you if you weren't there.'

'Our little secret.'

'Except for Mum and Dad.'

'Oh, I think they've forgotten about me. They don't worry any more.'

'I mention you sometimes and I see their faces.'

'Best not to disturb them.'

'I won't any more.'

A few days later Jon was having lunch with Mr Cohen, who outlined his plan for a European tour. He made his usual stipulation that Pam should accompany him, which was agreed although she herself had not yet been advised of the tour. As soon as the lunch was over he intended to go round to Manchester Square and tell her.

'We're off again, Pam,' he announced.

'As you thought,' she commented.

'Yes. Paris, Brussels, Berlin, Prague, Rome, Vienna.'

'That all?' asked Louise.

'What would you like from Paris, Mother?' asked Pam.

'I'll have to think, dear.'

'When do we start, Jon?'

'January.'

'Oh, good. I wouldn't want to be away at Christmas.'

'Neither would I.'

'You know, Jon,' remarked Louise, 'it's amazing to me that you still stay at home with Mary and Sam. I would have expected you to have set up your own pad in London.'

'I like my mother's cooking,' said Jon. 'If I didn't stay at home I'd want to stay with you. If you'd have me.'

'You'd be very welcome.'

'I have no liking for the so-called high life of parties and night clubs. I reckon I'm lazy. Father always said I was.'

'Huh!' scoffed Louise, being her assessment of her brother-in-law.

Mary was more tearful than usual when Jon left home for his European tour. The interval between tours had been so pleasant and relaxed that it was almost like the times when she used to look after him when he was at school. He played the piano continuously, of course, but he never seemed to want to go out. He phoned Pam regularly to talk about the new tour and reminisce about the earlier one. Occasionally he would drive the three of them into the country somewhere for an evening meal, but Sam wasn't all that keen on such excursions. He preferred to put his slippers on and watch television, but Mary knew that Jon did it to save her cooking. She enjoyed it.

Pam and Jon dutifully sent off greeting cards to their homes as they reached each city of the tour, which, as usual, was a great success.

They were holding a post mortem in their sitting room in the Hotel Sacher in Vienna, the last stage of the tour.

'I like Vienna,' said Jon.

'So do I,' agreed Pam. 'It seems to exude music.'

'I wonder what happens now.'

'How do you mean?'

'Do we do all the tours all over again?'

'I'm sure Mr Cohen will have thought of something.'

'It can't go on for ever. That's what Dad always said.'

'Not the same programme, of course. But you can vary that.'

'All the time they can bill me as "young", I suppose it will go on.'

'Good Heavens! What are you worrying about? You're famous, you're rich. You're not even middle-aged. You're not thinking of retiring, are you?'

'No. No.'

'You've got such a long face suddenly.'

'I'm thinking.'

'Oh.' Then, after a pause, 'Does that often happen?'

'You can laugh!'

'Someone's got to round here.'

'Shall I tell you what I was thinking?'

'Yes, please!'

'Do you realise you're the only girl I've ever known?'

'I didn't know that but I suspected it.'

'You're not only my wild oat you're my harvest.'

'Are you saying you want to do some more sowing?'

'No. I'm saying why don't we get married?'

'What!' exclaimed Pam, in horror.

'Why don't we get married?'

121

'That's what I thought you said.'
'Well?'
'Why?'
'Why not?'
'Why should we get married?'
'Why not?'
'I'm quite happy as I am, as we are. Aren't you?'
'Well, yes.'
'Well then.'
'I thought you'd like to get married.'
'I daresay I would.'
'Then why not?'
'I don't fancy leaving Mother on her own.'
'You've left her on her own quite a lot lately.'
'She's always known I'm coming back.'
'You could still go back after we're married.'
'It's not the same. Nothing of me or mine would be there. She'll know she was completely alone.'
'My mother's different, of course. There's Dad.'
'What made you think of marriage so suddenly?'
'It's not sudden. I've often thought of it.'
'Where would you live? Where would we live?'
'Where you like.'
'London?'
'To be near Mother?'
'In a way, yes.'
'I was thinking of the South of France.'
'A long way from Mr Cohen.'
'There's the telephone. A lot of concert people live abroad. Usually Italy.'
'That's because they happen to be Italian, dear.'
'So you're not keen?'
'I didn't say that.'
'You want me to go down on my knees?'
'Certainly not.'

'Alright. I'll ask you another time.'

'Thank you.'

The idea was forgotten in the turmoil of arrival at the airport and the flight to London Airport. A hire car had been laid on to take them to Pam's address, where they were welcomed by Aunt Louise. From there Jon picked up his own car and drove himself home. Once he had been greeted by his mother and the obligatory presents had been distributed, they were sitting at the kitchen table with a cup of tea when Jon said, 'When we were in Vienna I asked Pam to marry me.'

'Oh?'

'She didn't seem keen.'

'I expect she wants to think about it.'

'No. It's not that. I don't think she wants to leave Aunt Louise.'

'That's thoughtful of her.'

'Aunt Louise can last a long time, though.'

'So I should hope. You don't want to wish her dead, do you? She's my sister.'

'No. Of course not.'

'I don't suppose Pam would want her mother to live with you.'

'I don't know. If we found somewhere with a granny flat or an extension...'

'It's not a very good way to start a marriage. And I don't think Aunt Louise would want to leave her flat.'

'I didn't realise Pam was so attached to her mother. She's been away quite a lot lately.'

'Her mother's always known she was coming back.'

'That's just what Pam said. It's alright for you. You've got Dad.'

'We'd still miss you if you weren't here, dear.'

'You must know I'd get married sometime. All mothers must know that.'

'Of course. But, as you say, I have your father. Louise doesn't have anybody.'

'I wonder if Pam will tell her mother I asked her.'

'I wonder.'

They needn't have wondered. She did.

'Jon asked me to marry him,' said Pam.

'Oh! What did you say?' asked Louise.

'I put him off.'

'Why?'

'I need time to think.'

'I've never believed that old chant. Don't you like him?'

'Of course. It's not that.'

'What is it then? I'd like to see you married. You've been around my apron strings long enough.'

'But what would you do, Mother?'

'Well, you know I've often thought about that. I think I'd sell up here and move into a hotel.'

'A hotel?' echoed Pam, aghast.

'Yes. No cooking, no housework. Company if you want it. TV in your room.'

'You'd have nothing of your own round you.'

'Photos. I know some people who've done it. You have a sitting room where you can have your own bits and pieces but there's nothing I would want from here. The more I can sell, the longer I can stay in the hotel.'

'I don't like the sound of that, Mother.'

'You could visit, you see. It wouldn't be the Ritz, of course, but there are some nice hotels about that cater for that sort of thing. This is a good flat. It should make a good price.'

'It sounds as if you've been giving it a lot of thought.'

'I have. I thought of it after your father died but you were here.'

'So I'm the one who's been holding you back, and I thought I couldn't leave you alone.'

'Yes. So there's no need to put Jon off, you see.'

'He may not ask me again.'

'Of course he will. If he doesn't, then he didn't mean it in the first place.'

'Mother! You're a wonder!' exclaimed Pam, throwing her arms round her neck and kissing her.

In her exuberance Pam rang Jon that evening, but Mary answered.

'Oh, hello, Aunt,' said Pam, without enthusiasm.

'Hello, Pam. Did you enjoy the tour?'

'Very much.'

'Where will it be next?'

'That's up to the Maestro.'

'Did you want to speak to him?'

'Yes, please.'

'Hold on.'

Mary put the phone down and called up the stairs to Jon's room.

'Jon!'

Jon came to the door. 'Yes?'

'Pam on the phone.'

'Right.'

He hurried down the stairs and picked up the phone.

'Hello.'

'Hello, Maestro. Do you still want to marry me?'

'Of course.'

'Then the answer's yes.'

Jon was silent. He sat down on the stairs.

'You still there?' asked Pam.

'Yes.'

'It's the lady who's supposed to faint, not the man.'

'I'm sorry. I was a bit overwhelmed. I'd told Mother you turned me down.'

'I'll tell you all the details when I see you, but evidently Mother fancies living in a hotel and is only waiting for me to leave.'

'Well I'm damned.'

'You will be, dear, if you marry me,' Pam laughingly proclaimed.

'I'll risk that.'

'Love you, dear.'

'Love you.'

Jon stood motionless after putting the phone down. Then he returned slowly to the sitting room to join his mother.

'That was Pam,' he said.

'Yes, I know. I spoke to her.'

'She says she'll marry me after all.'

'Well, aren't you pleased? You don't look it.'

'I'm a bit stunned. I thought she'd said no.'

'A lady is allowed to change her mind.'

'Evidently Aunt Louise wants to live in a hotel somewhere.'

'Oh, she's always been on about that.'

'Has she?'

'She likes the idea of doing nothing and being looked after. No housework, no cooking. It's been her hobby horse since her husband died. She always said she'd like to press a bell and have breakfast in bed.'

'Good luck to her.'

'And good luck to you, dear. Pam's a nice girl.'

'Yes. She is.'

'I must say I thought you'd marry some celebrity.'

'Whatever for?'

'You move in those circles.'

'Not me.'

'Where do you think you'll live?'

'No idea. I thought of the South of France but I don't think Pam's keen.'

'It's a long way away.'

'Not these days. There's the telephone.'

'I expect Pam would like London. She's used to it.'

'Yes. I suppose I could get used to it.'

'It would be nice if you were near.'

'Yes, I know. I think I'll go and play.'

In a somewhat sombre frame of mind Jon went into the front room to play the piano. He was sombre because he felt he had made a major step in his life and although it was his own choosing, he nevertheless worried that he could carry it off. He had no financial problems. He was actually quite rich. He loved Pam and he was convinced that they would get on very well together, so why wasn't he leaping in the air? He didn't know why. What he did know was that he wanted to be with Pam right now, to talk to her. The telephone wasn't enough.

While she was listening to her son playing in the front room, Mary was wondering what she should wear for the wedding. It was bound to be one of those fashionable affairs, she presumed. It was all very well for Sam. He could hire a suit. Perhaps she could, too. She'd ask somebody, though she felt sure that Jon would help her with the expense if necessary. She would need a hat. She hadn't worn a hat for years. She suddenly felt happy though she knew she would miss Jon being at home.

When Mary imagined a well publicised wedding she was only half correct. Two leading picture magazines began bidding for the right to photograph the event. Jon and Pam discussed it as they drove down to the New Forest for a break – Pam's favourite part of the world – staying at Chewton Glen on the way.

'I don't fancy a lavish affair, do you?' asked Jon.

'Lord, no,' agreed Pam. 'The affair's not your own then.'

Already the media was splashing their names about. 'PIANIST COUSINS TO WED', they proclaimed. Neither Jon nor Pam had given any interviews, yet the newspapers practised their guesswork and for the most part they were not wrong. However, Jon had not proposed in Paris, he'd proposed in Vienna, and the wedding was not to take place in Westminster but at St George's, Hanover Square. The bride was given away by her uncle, Sam Stern, in place of her absent father. Both mothers cried. The reception was at the Dorchester. The happy couple spent their honeymoon in the Caribbean, all of which was accompanied by the usual publicity.

Mary Stern collected all she could of the cuttings and photographs, not only of the wedding, and spent many sentimental hours pasting them into a scrapbook to join all the other cuttings she had amassed covering Jon's tours and recitals. Often when she was alone she would sit at the kitchen table and turn the pages, shedding a few tears as she did so.

It was while Jon and Pam were on their honeymoon that Jenni spoke to Jon without any prompting. It happened in the bathroom after their first night at the hotel.

'I'll be leaving you now, Jon,' said Jenni.

Jon swung round in alarm to face the sound.

'What! Jenni, you can't!' cried Jon.

'You don't need me now.'

'I do. I do.'

'Not now you're married. Pam will take my place.'

'She can't. She doesn't know how to. Don't leave me, Jenni. Please.'

'There is nothing more I can do.'

'There is. There is. I need you all the time.'

'You're rich and famous now.'

'That doesn't matter. We've always been friends. You helped me at school. You're part of me.'

'I'm sorry, Jon, but it's goodbye.'

'No! No!'

Jon moved about the room as if searching.

'Oh, God, Jenni. Tell me where you are, Jenni.'

'It doesn't matter where I am. You mustn't rely on my kind of help now. Pam will help you.'

'Jenni! Jenni! Don't leave me.'

'It's time, Jon.'

'Time for what? I don't understand. Come back.'

'No.'

'Jenni!'

'Goodbye, Jon.'

'No!'

Jon's cry of entreaty was followed by a complete silence as if in a vacuum. He collapsed in a chair beside the bath and burst into tears. He held his head in his hands and sobbed uncontrollably.

Pam, wondering what was keeping Jon so long, entered the bathroom without knocking. She was shocked to see Jon with his head in his hands sobbing.

'Jon!' she cried. 'Whatever's the matter?'

Suddenly disturbed in his grief, Jon jumped up and brushed the back of his hands across his eyes.

'Nothing. I'm alright,' he said.

'It's the bride who's supposed to cry after the wedding night, not the groom.'

'It's nothing. Really.'

Jon pushed his way back to the bedroom, where he fell on the bed, eyes closed. Pam stood beside him.

'You're a bundle of emotions, I must say,' she

soothed. 'I should know. I've been on all your tours. But this is new.'

'I'm alright, I tell you,' snapped Jon, without looking at her.

In his grief over the loss of Jenni, Jon was inclined to be short-tempered and testy. Pam noticed it. She was puzzled. Only a few moments ago they were so intimately relaxed. Why was he crying in the bathroom? And she was convinced that he was. Was it his loss of freedom through marriage or a reflex action after so much performing on the concert platform? It couldn't be either of these things, Pam decided, because that was just not like Jon. She would never know and she would never ask him.

For the rest of the day and forever after Jon behaved as if nothing had happened and Pam decided to leave well alone. She felt sure that he would tell her if he was concerned about anything. The tears could have been extreme tiredness. That evening at dinner Jon said, 'I've been thinking.'

'Yes?'

'I have an idea.'

'Yes?'

'You remember when I first came to your flat?'

'Yes.'

'We played together.'

'Are you speaking musically?'

'We played duets.'

'That's right.'

'Bartok duets.'

'I remember.'

'What do you think of the idea of our touring the duets?'

'Both of us?'

'Yes.'

'It's alright for you, dear. You're established. I'm not.'

'You're very good. You play very well. We'd be good together. We could do it.'

'But I've never done any concert work. I'm not known.'

'You'll be known as Pamela Stern.'

'I could never memorise all that Bartok.'

'We'll have page turners.'

'Turners? Plural?'

'Yes. We'll use two pianos.'

'That's expensive for the concert people.'

'It will be impressive.'

'What will Mr Cohen say?'

'I should think he'll be pleased. Otherwise it's just me going round and round again.'

'Which is as it should be.'

'Don't you like the idea?'

'I think it's a wonderful idea but I doubt if I could live up to it.'

'Of course you can.'

'You might think so but will Mr Cohen?'

'He'll fall for the husband and wife team. The publicity.'

'You've got it all worked out, haven't you?'

With a big grin Jon simply said, 'Yes.'

Then why the tears and sobbing, thought Pam. She wanted to ask but daren't. It must remain a mystery until Jon was prepared to explain himself. The tears were real enough. Pam was sure of that.

Mr Cohen thought that Jon's idea was a good one and was not slow to appreciate the publicity value of the venture immediately the press and television picked up the story and exploited it. The interviewing and personal appearances were new to Pam. She found it all

131

a little frightening but Jon took it all in his stride. Both mothers, Mary and Louise, were excited by the idea of their children appearing on the concert platform together. Jon Stern evidently believed in putting his wife to work, commented one critic.

The venue for the first recital was at the Barbican in London. The two grand pianos with the name *Steinway* blazoned on the sides had pride of place on the platform. Jon and Pam were followed onto the stage at a discreet distance by two young male students acting as page turners. Pam wore a voluminous scarlet dress off the shoulders, exposing an inviting bosom. She looked very attractive and complemented the handsome Jon in his white tie and tails.

Although Bartok may not have been everyone's favourite composer, the idea of husband and wife duettists attracted a full house. Louise and Mary as the respective mothers beamed proudly as their offspring performed. Poor Sam was completely at a loss with this kind of music. He could find nothing to hum. To him it was mere cacophony and he was bored. The only thing that intrigued him was the attitude of the page turners. He wouldn't have expected them to stand at the side of the piano that they did. He thought that they should be on the other side.

The recital was a great success and even the critics were enthusiastic, if only to show off their musical erudition. At the end of the recital Jon turned to Pam.

'You see? You needn't have worried. You appeared on the platform as if you'd been doing it all your life.'

'I'm glad it's over, though,' confessed Pam.

'It's not over, dear,' Jon warned her. 'It's only just started.'

As a result of the Barbican recital Mr Cohen organised a British tour prior to Europe, and this time

Pam and Jon were able to share the same bedroom officially, thus saving expense.

After a series of provincial hotel bedroom suites and in spite of the enormous success of the tour, Jon and Pam were glad to escape to their apartment in Monte Carlo, which had become a bolt hole. They had a house in London but it was rarely free of telephone calls or personal callers. At Monte Carlo they could relax by the sea and drive anywhere along the coast, and there was always the Symphony Orchestra to listen to at the Casino. They had come to know some of the musicians and conductors.

While Jon and Pam were relaxing in Monte Carlo Mr Cohen, encouraged by the provincial success of the duettists, was busy organising a European tour for the Bartok venture.

Again Pam and Jon played on two pianos with a slight difference. This time the page turners were girl students. The first concert was in Paris, of course. Pam's page turner was an ordinary, pleasant looking girl of about eighteen years of age, but Jon's was a pretty girl of similar age with an attractive figure. Jon and Pam made private jokes about the girl, though both girls were very efficient and contributed to pleasant teamwork. They were not to know, until their next destination, that Mr Cohen had arranged for the same two French girl page turners to accompany the duettists throughout the tour. This avoided the possibility of John and Pam being put off by the introduction of strangers to the team.

After Paris came Brussels, Rome, and a whole list of European capital cities, ending with the final concert in Vienna. Each concert achieved more acclaim than the other as they progressed on the tour. In Vienna they enjoyed the comfort of a spacious suite in the Hotel Sacher, opposite the New Opera House. Pam spent the afternoon shopping while Jon lounged in the sitting room resting. Pam spent a long time shopping and when she returned to the hotel suite she was shocked to see Jon in bed with Michelle, his page turner.

'Jon!' she shrieked.

At once the girl scrambled out of the bed and hurriedly put her clothes on.

'Sorry. So sorry,' she muttered and ran out of the room.

Jon had no chance to say anything to Pam because she turned on her heel and went out of the bedroom to the sitting room.

'Pam!' cried Jon, hurrying after her.

Pam was retrieving her suitcase from the lounge and taking it into the bedroom where she started packing.

'Pam, I'm sorry. I don't know what came over me.'

'It's pretty obvious what came over you,' retorted Pam, throwing clothes into her case.

'What are you doing?' asked Jon.

'Packing.'

'What for?'

'I'm going home.'

'You can't do that!'

'I can and I will.'

She picked up the telephone and spoke to the concierge.

'Mrs Stern. Will you get me on a plane to London as soon as possible, please?'

She waited a moment.

'When? Two hours. Thank you. Will you send up for my suitcases?'

'Pam! You can't! We've got a concert tonight.'

'You may have. I haven't.'

'Pam! You can't let the audience down.'

'You're the one who's letting them down.'

'Can't we talk it over?'

'No. Actions speak louder than words and I've seen enough.'

Further argument was interrupted by the ringing of the door bell. Half naked as he was, Jon opened the door. It was the porter for Pam's luggage. Jon let him in.

'It's the porter,' he announced.

'Just finished,' Pam called out from the bedroom.

The porter entered the bedroom and took away two suitcases.

'Is the taxi here?' asked Pam.

'Yes, madam,' replied the porter.

Once the porter had left the suite Jon pleaded again.

'Pam. Please.'

'No, Jon. It's no good.'

'It was only a lapse.'

'Goodbye.'

'Where are you going?'

'I told you. Home. I'm not staying here a minute longer.'

'How can I reach you?'

'I'd rather you didn't.'

'Let me come to the airport with you.'

'No!'

'Pam!'

He followed her to the lift, pleading, but Pam did not say another word. As she descended in the lift Jon wailed, 'Pam!'

Sadly he returned to the suite. It was now tea time but he went at once to the drinks cabinet and poured himself a whisky. Then another.

Rumours soon filled the air. Pam Stern was seen leaving the hotel with two suitcases and boarding a plane for London. The newsmen were not slow to ask questions. The tour manager's office was flooded with calls. The concert officials were also asking questions.

The tour manager, James Oliver, was a small, round, bespectacled man of middle age, accustomed to fawning on celebrities. He was unable to answer the questions coming over the phone so he decided to call Jon at the hotel.

The phone rang in Jon's sitting room but he took a long time to answer it.

'Hello,' he said, with a slight slur.

'Mr Stern. James Oliver here.'

'Yes? What do you want?'

'I've been inundated with calls saying that Mrs Stern has gone back to London. Is that right?'

Jon, in his maudlin state, did not know what to say. There was a silence on the phone.

'Mr Stern. Are you there?' urged Mr Oliver.

'She's not feeling very well,' moaned Jon, eventually.

'Does that mean we'll have to cancel tonight's concert or will she be back in time?'

'No. No. Don't cancel. Say the programme's changed. Instead of duets I'll go on alone.'

'Are you sure? I mean, do you feel up to it?'

James Oliver was anxious about Jon's strange behaviour. He had to admit that the man sounded drunk.

'Of course I'm up to it,' protested Jon.

'Can I tell them what you'll be playing?'

'No. I don't know myself yet.'

'I see. Right. I'll get that news out straight away.'

When Jon put the phone down he poured himself yet another drink. He did not realise how much he was drinking or how drunk he was becoming.

There was a buzz of anticipation in the concert hall that night and a group of newsmen were waiting at the stage door when Jon arrived.

'How is your wife, Mr Stern?' one of them called out.

'When will your wife be back, Mr Stern?' asked another.

Jon pushed his way through the throng without saying a word and made his way to his dressing room, where the tour manager was waiting for him.

'Oh, hello, James,' said Jon, a little flippantly.

'There's all sorts of rumours flying around I'm afraid,' announced Mr Oliver.

'Really?'

Jon attempted to change into his white tie and tails and seemed to have some difficulty balancing on one leg to get his trousers on. James Oliver studied him closely. Jon was behaving oddly, he thought. Could it be concern for his wife? He could smell whisky on his breath and it worried him.

'There's talk that you had a quarrel,' said James Oliver.

'Quarrel? Who with?'

'Your wife.'

'Rubbish.'

'I thought you should know what people are saying.'

'Of course.'

'Hotel gossip, most of it. They say your wife was in a furious temper when she left.'

Jon didn't answer. Instead he asked, 'Is there any drink in the place?'

'Of course,' replied James Oliver, and went at once to the cocktail cabinet. 'Did you want a Coke or something?'

'Any Scotch?'

'Scotch?' James sounded incredulous.

'Pour me one.'

James Oliver had never known Jon to be in such a strange humour.

'Soda or water?' he asked.

'As it is.'

'Do you think you should? Before a concert?'

'I can play it backwards.'

Against his better judgement, James Oliver dutifully poured a small Scotch in a glass and handed it to Jon, who gulped it down and coughed for some time, excusing himself profusely. James Oliver felt sure that Jon was not in a condition to perform.

'Don't you think I should make some excuses and cancel the concert?' he suggested.

'Don't be a bloody fool!'

Jon looked at his wrist watch.

'Time. Come on.'

James Oliver followed Jon out of the dressing room. Jon made his way in quite a determined manner to the stage. James Oliver remained in the wings. There were two pianos on the stage as duettists were expected. Jon moved to the centre of the stage and looked first at one piano and then the other.

'I can only play one at a time,' he said.

The remark was greeted with a certain amount of laughter.

'In the absence of my wife,' Jon went on, 'who unfortunately has retired sick, I will endeavour to entertain you with piano solos.'

The news was welcomed by applause but not in the volume that it should have been. Jon turned from the audience and went to the piano on the right of the stage, the one that he would have been playing if Pam had joined him. He took a little time settling on the stool and arranging himself. James Oliver, watching from the wings in a state of anxiety, imagined that Jon would revert to his original programme, and he was right.

As soon as he was settled, Jon crashed into the Rachmaninoff prelude. He took it at a faster tempo than usual and seemed to put all his anger and frustration into it. To James Oliver's relief he didn't play any wrong notes and if he hadn't known that it was not Jon's usual interpretation he would have still considered it a superb performance. Jon went off the stage without bowing to the audience in spite of the enthusiastic applause. He went directly to his dressing room and poured himself a neat Scotch. James Oliver stood at the doorway, watching.

'Do you think you should?' he warned once again.

Jon put the empty glass down on the table and made his way back to the stage, ignoring the manager. Once at the piano he settled himself again and began to play Liszt's *La Camponile*. This required a great deal of concentration and precise fingering and James Oliver noticed that while Jon was playing he was perspiring profusely, something he had never done before. At the end of the piece there was thunderous applause because the playing called for a certain amount of pianistic histrionics. Again Jon left the piano without acknowledging the audience. Again he went directly to his dressing room, where he drank another whisky.

'Mr Stern,' pleaded James Oliver, 'you're taking a great risk.'

'Then I'm taking it, not you,' snapped Jon as he made his way back to the platform, striding confidently to the piano.

In the wings James Oliver felt some relief that Jon was about to embark on the final piece, the simpler, softer, not all that difficult Liszt's *Consolation.* Jon had played it so often and so beautifully that it had become his trademark. Unfortunately, as so often happens when people indulge in too much alcohol, the simplest

139

sentence or movement can be their undoing, and so it happened with the *Consolation*. Jon somehow got into trouble with the left hand, the crucial element of the music. He stumbled to such an extent that he had to go over one section again just as if he were a student practicing the piece for the first time. The audience groaned so much that it caused Jon to panic. He never completed the item, got up and left the platform in a hurry, the booing and catcalls of the audience ringing in his ears.

In the dressing room, as Jon was changing his clothes, the manager turned on him.

'You've done it now,' declared James Oliver. 'That's the end.'

'End of what?'

'Your career, I'd say.'

'So what?'

'Don't you care?'

'All I care about at the moment is getting home to Pam. Get me on the first plane you can and let me know at the hotel.'

'What about...?' James Oliver began.

'What about nothing.'

'The press.'

'You deal with them. That's your job.'

'God knows what the critics will say.'

Jon did not wait to hear any more. He strode out of the room with the manager following him.

'You may have trouble at the stage door,' he warned.

'I'm not speaking to anyone,' declared Jon.

There was quite a crowd at the stage door, a few anxious fans among the newspapermen.

'What happened, Mr Stern?' one of the newsmen called out.

'How's your wife, Mr Stern?'

'When's the next concert, Mr Stern?'

With the physical help of James Oliver and the chauffeur, Jon managed to get into his car and was driven away. Poor James Oliver was left surrounded by a crowd of people clamouring for news.

Jon was aware of the strange glances of the hotel staff as he made his way to the lift. Once in his suite he fell into the nearest armchair and burst into tears.

'That won't help,' said a voice near Jon.

Jon jumped to his feet.

'Jenni!' he cried, eagerly. 'You're back?'

'Yes, you little fool.'

'I know. I'm sorry.'

'The trouble is you've only known one girl, and that's Pam. When the little page turner came along you couldn't resist.'

'Pam needn't have run off as she did,' complained Jon.

'Don't blame her. Blame yourself.'

'I know.'

'You know you can't drink. You've never liked it. What did you do that for?'

'I don't know.'

'What are you going to do now?'

'I'm going to try and get Pam back.'

'What about your career?'

'Pam is more important.'

'Then tell her so.'

'I don't know where she is.'

'Her mother will know. Apart from that, I think you should make a public confession to save yourself'

'How do you mean?'

'When you get back to London you'll be met by the usual crowd of newspeople.'

'I expect so, yes.'

'Tell them you want to make a full statement. But not at the airport. Make a date for some hotel.'

'I'll get that organised, yes.'

'Admit that you were found in bed with your page turner. Admit that when Pam walked out, which she had every right to do, you started to drink and you're not very good at it. Admit that when you appeared at the concert you were drunk. Promise that it will never happen again, and even if it means the end of your career Pam is more important to you and you would do anything to get her back.'

'I see.'

'Can you remember all that?'

'Oh, yes. Because it's what I feel.'

'Good.'

'Thank you for coming back, Jenni.'

'I had to. You were in trouble.'

'I'm sorry. It was all my fault.'

'I hope you won't need me again.'

'I'll try not to but it's nice to know you're still somewhere.'

'Goodbye, Jon.'

'Goodbye, Jenni.'

Jon naturally felt sad that Jenni had to go away again but he also felt elated and uplifted to know that she was still near. The parting was not the harrowing grief that he suffered when she first left him because he now knew that she was never far away. She had become a part of him and, spirit or not, she was very real to him. There were a few tears at the new parting but they were tears of affection, warm tears of love at parting.

He picked up the telephone and put a call through to London in the hope of speaking to Aunt Louise. He was connected immediately.

'Aunt Louise?'

'Yes.'

'Jon.'

'Where are you?'

'Vienna.

'How are you?'

'Fine. I mean no, I'm not. Is Pam with you?'

'At the moment, yes.'

'What does that mean?'

'Well, there isn't room for her to stay here.'

'Can I speak to her?'

'I'd say yes if she wanted to speak to you, but she doesn't.'

'Oh.'

'You've been a bit of a bloody fool, haven't you?'

'I'm afraid so. I wanted to tell her.'

'Have you seen the papers?'

'No. But I'm sure they're having a field day.'

'Concert pianist too drunk to play. Concert pianist leaves platform staggering. Concert pianist booed. And a lot more besides. Doesn't look as if you'll ever play again, dear.'

'It doesn't, does it.'

'I hope you've saved your pennies.'

'I'm not worried about that. Will you tell Pam I rang?'

'She's sitting beside me. She can hear me speaking to you.'

'Tell her–'

Aunt Louise interrupted. 'Leave it, Jon. Leave it.'

'Alright. Sorry to trouble you.'

'No trouble. 'Bye.'

''Bye.'

Jon's next call was from his mother, who, to avoid trouble with Sam, had reversed the charges.

'Hello, Mother.'

'Jon! What on earth is going on?' she asked, anxiously.

'Nothing now, Mother. I've put up a bit of black but I'm hoping to repair the damage.'

'Your father was furious when he read the papers.'

'I can imagine.'

'It's not very nice, let's face it.'

'It's nothing criminal, Mother.'

'You've ruined yourself.'

'It looks like it.'

'I hope you've saved some money.'

'I'm not worried about that. The most important thing is to get Pam back.'

'Pam can't help your career, which is over now.'

'Don't say that, Mother.'

'Well, it is, isn't it?'

'Let's say it would appear so.'

'A brilliant career ruined by a silly little chit of a girl.'

'That's how it's happened through the ages.'

'You can't afford to be flippant, Jon.'

'I can always take up teaching pupils at home.'

'Jon!'

'Don't keep on, Mother. I'll be back tomorrow. We can talk then.'

'Very well.'

'Goodbye, Mother.'

Mary didn't answer. She put the phone down, leaving Jon to make an all-important call to Mr Cohen.

'Are you mad?' was Mr Cohen's opening remark. 'I can't book you anywhere at the moment, Jon. You just don't exist.'

'I'm not surprised,' Jon admitted. 'But I have a solution. At least I think it could be a solution.'

'I'll be pleased to hear it.'

Jon outlined his plans as prompted by Jenni. He asked Mr Cohen if he could arrange, through his manager, a photo-call, which Jon was prepared to pay for.

'What good do you think that will do?' asked Mr Cohen.

'Probably none but it's worth a try.'

'A photo-call?' echoed Mr Cohen, in amazement.

'I'll talk to the press. Not just pictures.'

'They're not very fond of you at the moment, Jon.'

'I know. But I hope to sort them out.'

'Good luck. That's all I can say.'

The date for the press conference was fixed for the time of Jon's arrival from Vienna. To all those newsmen who pursued him at the airport he called out, 'See you at the Dorchester!'

At which they all hurried to their cars.

At a conference room in the Dorchester refreshments were laid on for the press at midday. Gilt chairs were arranged for those who wanted to use them and a table with a microphone was set up at the head of the room with one chair set by it.

There was a large assembly of newsmen and photographers and the babble of conversation was almost deafening. The noise was suddenly quelled when Jon appeared and sat at the table.

'Good morning, gentlemen. And ladies. I beg your pardon. I mean ladies and gentlemen. My name is Jon Stern, otherwise known as the bloody fool.'

The audience laughed happily, making notes.

'It was all my fault,' Jon went on. 'I've dropped a brick, made a bloomer, put up a black, whatever you like to call it. Everything was going smoothly in Vienna. We were having a lovely time. It's a marvellous city. Until my wife went shopping. Nothing exceptional in that, of course. But when she got back she found me in bed. And I wasn't alone.'

The audience laughed and gasped in mock horror.

'Who was she?' asked one of the audience.

'I don't think it would be fair to mention names,' declared Jon. 'I'm sure you could find out if you wanted to. The poor girl scuttled away and it would be a shame if the incident damaged her career as it has probably done mine. I owe her an apology. I also owe my wife an apology. She didn't scuttle away exactly. She just left. And I haven't seen her since. I hope that she will forgive me and come back and play duets with me again. I must also apologise to the audience in Vienna. I'm afraid that when my wife walked out I turned to the bottle and I'm not used to it. Perhaps some of you here could teach me.'

'Any time!' called out several voices.

'I managed one or two pieces on the piano. Not my best efforts, and I came to grief on Liszt's beautiful *Consolation,* a not particularly difficult piece. And that, ladies and gentlemen, is my story and I'm stuck with it. Any questions?'

Of course there were questions and they all came at once.

'One at a time, please,' insisted Jon. 'Ladies first.'

One of the ladies stood up.

'What are you going to do now, Mr Stern?' she asked.

'First of all I will do all I can to get my wife back. She's the most important.'

'Will you go on playing?' asked another lady. 'Or do you consider your career at an end?'

'I hope to go on playing and I hope that my career, such as it is, is not at an end. But I am in the hands of the public. If anyone will have me after my terrible behaviour in Vienna I will be very grateful. But I would like to continue playing with my wife. If you understand me.'

146

The last remark produced a titter among the audience.

'Would you consider playing duets with someone else?' asked a newsman.

'No,' replied Jon, promptly.

'Why not?'

'It's not a question of why not. My wife and I are a team. I can't tell you what a wonderful feeling it is to sit facing her across the stage from our two pianos. It's a kind of affinity. I do hope she comes back so that we can do it again.'

Another male journalist stood up.

'Even if your wife did come back,' he said, 'can you be sure you'd be able to play duets again?'

'You mean, will we be wanted?' Jon prompted.

'Exactly.'

'That I can't say. I can only hope.'

'So your career is in the balance?'

'I'm afraid so.'

'You're in trouble, aren't you, sir?' declared one of the newsmen.

'Deep trouble,' admitted Jon. 'I can only blame myself. I repeat: I was a bloody fool. If they will have me and if my wife comes back, I'm prepared to give a concert in Vienna free of charge. But don't tell my agent.'

After an appreciative laugh he added, 'I'll have to pay the wife, of course.'

'And the page turner?' asked a newsman.

'I've already paid for that,' said Jon.

He stood up, indicating that the session was over.

'I'd now like to join you in a non-alcoholic drink,' he declared.

The crush and noisy chatter of the media types soon made inroads into the food and drink.

'Where are you going from here, Mr Stern?' one of the newsmen asked Jon.

'You mean, when I leave here?'

'Yes.'

'I'm going to try to find my wife.'

'Have you any idea where she is?'

'Oh, yes.'

'I'd like to cover the reunion.'

'If you do that, I doubt if there will be a reunion.'

'Oh.'

'So would you mind giving it a miss?'

'OK.'

'Thanks.'

In spite of their promises, one or two of the newsmen followed Jon from the Dorchester Hotel to the hotel where Pam's mother was living. He knew the number of the mini-suite and, ignoring the lift, raced up the stairs and along the corridor. He rang the bell. The door was opened by Pam herself.

'Oh!' exclaimed Jon.

He did not know what to say or do. Pam looked really lovely, he thought, and wanted to tell her so but decided it might sound insincere in the circumstances.

'Did you want to see my mother?' asked Pam.

'No. I want to see you.'

'Well, you're looking at me.'

'May I come in?'

'This is not my apartment.'

'Will you ask your mother if I can come in?'

At that moment Jon heard Aunt Louise call out.

'Who is it, dear?'

'Jon,' replied Pam.

'Oh!' cried Louise happily as she ran to the door.

'Come in! Come in!' she urged.

Jon entered the apartment and Pam closed the door.

Louise led Jon into the sitting room. The apartment consisted of a bedroom, sitting room, bathroom and cupboard kitchen.

'Put the kettle on, Pam,' instructed Louise.

'If he's staying to tea then I'm going out,' threatened Pam.

Jon was startled by his wife's reaction.

'That would be very rude of you, dear,' admonished Louise, 'when I invite someone to tea.'

'Pam,' began Jon. 'I came here to apologise and beg your forgiveness. I've just done a television interview admitting that I was a bloody fool, and that will go out to several million viewers, including you. I made it quite clear that you mean more to me than even my career, which is probably blown away. I said it on television and I meant it, as I mean it now. I was an idiot. A fool.'

'Words, words,' muttered Pam.

'Oh dear,' sighed Jon. 'I don't want to argue with you. I love you, Pam. I always have and always will. I never want to hurt you, ever. What happened will never, never, never happen again.'

'I should hope not,' commented Pam.

'If you two are going to argue,' declared Aunt Louise, 'I'll put the kettle on myself.'

'I'll do it, Aunt,' offered Jon as he went to the small kitchen in the corridor.

'You don't have to play hard to get, dear,' whispered Aunt Louise to her daughter.

'I'm not.'

'He's said he's sorry. You'll be a fool if you don't go back to him.'

'Oh, I'll go back.'

'He can't have much of a future now. Letting the audience down like that in Vienna.'

'He's still a fantastic pianist.'

149

'Do you think he can get back?'

'I don't know. Only Mr Cohen can tell you that.'

'When will you tell him?'

'After his television show tonight.'

'Why then?'

'Mother, there are newsmen outside the hotel. If our reconciliation happened before his TV show, any possibility of his redeeming himself to his public will be wasted. They'd probably not show the clip.'

'I see what you mean. That's clever of you.'

Jon returned to the sitting room carrying a tray of three decorative mugs of tea.

'I hope I've done it properly,' he said. 'Yours is on the right, Aunt.'

'Oh, thank you, dear.'

Aunt Louise took her mug of tea from the tray.

'Darling.'

Jon proffered the tray to Pam.

'Thank you.'

Jon put the tray aside and sat down with his own mug of tea.

'Cheers,' he said.

After they'd tasted their tea Aunt Louise asked, 'What happens now, Jon?'

'I wish I knew,' admitted Jon. 'I'll get in touch with Mr Cohen but the last time I spoke to him he wasn't very helpful. I'll probably end up giving piano lessons in the front room.'

'You haven't got a front room,' chided Pam.

'I'll probably end up with one.'

'When we married you were rich and famous.'

'And now I'm not so rich, and infamous.'

'For richer or poorer,' quoted Aunt Louise.

'Don't remind me,' moaned Pam.

'And all because of a one-off,' said Jon.

'You mean one-on, don't you?' suggested Pam.

'If the worst comes to the worst I could sell the place in Monte Carlo.'

'Don't you dare!' cried Pam.

'No?'

'No. I like that place.'

'I thought that's where you'd be now, actually.'

'Oh, no,' put in Aunt Louise. 'When the bride runs away she comes to Mother.'

'Have you made up your mind, Pam?' asked Jon.

'If it's any interest to you, Jon,' replied Pam, 'I've been very unhappy without you and can't wait for us to get back together again.'

'Really?' exclaimed Jon.

'Really,' echoed Pam.

'Darling!'

Jon leapt out of his chair, fell on his knees in front of Pam, grabbed her round the waist and buried his face in her bosom. Pam's mug of tea fell out of her hand, the contents spilling onto her dress.

'My dress!' she cried.

'Fuck your dress,' said Jon.

'I'll get a towel,' declared Aunt Louise, calm and practical.

'Bless you, dearest,' murmured Jon. 'Can we go home now?'

'No.'

'What!'

'Listen, dear. There are newsmen out front. I don't want them to see us reunited until after your TV show.'

'Why?'

'Because whatever you've said could be lost and all your efforts to win back your audience wasted.'

'Ah, yes. I see what you mean.'

'I take it you apologised to Vienna.'

'Profusely.'

'Then we don't want to spoil that.'

'So I'll leave here on my own, giving the impression that there's been no reconciliation.'

'That's it. And I'll come over to you after the TV.'

'Good.'

Aunt Louise came into the room with a towel and began to mop at Pam's dress.

'I'll do it,' said Pam, taking the towel from her mother.

When Jon left the hotel he made no comment to the few newsmen waiting outside, hoping that his straight face would give the impression that all was not well with his marriage. As he drove away they dispersed because they had no idea whether Pam was in the building or not.

Jon waited in his house in Avenue Road for Pam to come back to him. In the meantime he watched the television interview. Pam and Aunt Louise watched it at the same time. Pam laughed a lot but Aunt Louise was worried.

'It's very clever,' she commented. 'He's certainly humbled himself.'

'Let's hope they see it in Vienna,' said Pam.

'Yes. That's important.'

'It's a very disarming confession.'

'I wonder what Mr Cohen will think of it.'

'There are other agents if he doesn't want to keep him on.'

Later that evening Jon opened the front door to Pam.

'Darling!' he cried.

As soon as she was in the hall Jon held her in a tight embrace.

152

'You're a plausible bastard, I must say,' Pam declared.

They didn't wait to go upstairs. They hurried into the sitting room and started to undress each other. Having made passionate love, they fell breathless onto one of the sofas.

As they began to dress, Pam remarked, 'You really were frightened, weren't you?'

'Frightened?'

'That I was going to leave you.'

'Christ, yes.'

'I wouldn't do that.'

'You had me worried.'

'You had me in a filthy temper for a long time. I thought I'd never forgive you.'

'I know. I'm sorry.'

'You say that very easily, sorry.'

'There's nothing else I can say. Nothing else I can feel. I don't know of any other word.'

'Then let's forget it.'

'Yes. Let's.'

Once they were fully dressed and in the right mind, as the saying goes, Pam could not resist asking, 'What was she like?'

'You said forget it.'

'I still want to know what she was like.'

'I've no idea.'

'What?'

'We had just started when you came in.'

Pam laughed so helplessly that she fell back on the sofa. When she recovered she announced, 'If we ever do any more duets we'll have male page turners.'

'I'm glad you said it.'

'Aren't you going to ring Mr Cohen?'

'I don't think I dare. He wasn't very pleased about the photo-call. I think he's finished with me.'

'Never mind. Let's go down to Monte Carlo and enjoy ourselves.'

'Good idea.'

The next morning was devoted to packing, interrupted by the arrival of the newspapers, which Jon handed to Pam.

'You see what they say. I daren't look,' he said.

Pam inspected the headlines. She began to recite, 'Ingenious genius. Jon Stern completely disarmed us. Of course we forgive him. He has a talent apart from his music. Full speed a-Stern. We won't forgive him if he doesn't play again. Not much wrong with that,' said Pam.

'Lucky,' commented Jon.

'That'll go round the world I expect,' said Pam.

'I hope it goes to Vienna.'

'Sure to. They're the ones who suffered.'

'I wonder what their reaction will be.'

'If you keep to your offer of a free recital, I should think they'd jump at it.'

'That recital's for duets.'

'I know.'

At that moment the telephone rang. Jon answered it.

'Hello … Speaking … Yes of course … What time? … I'll be there.'

'Where will you be?' asked Pam, as Jon put the phone down.

'That was Mr Cohen's secretary.'

'Oh.'

'He wants to see me in his office at midday today.'

'If he doesn't want to handle you any more, he could have told you that on the phone.'

'He obviously wants to talk about the TV and press business.'

'He's not the only agent, darling.'

'He's the best. You said so.'

'He is.'

'I could always sell my story to the newspapers, I suppose. So could you.'

'We're still going to Monte Carlo? I hope I'm not packing for nothing?'

'Of course.'

Jon went out of his way to look smart when he presented himself at Mr Cohen's office. He wore a blue suit with a white shirt and a striped tie. Pam approved his appearance, adding a white handkerchief to his breast pocket.

'Good morning, Mr Stern,' greeted Mr Cohen's secretary, without smiling. 'Just a minute.'

Jon stood by her desk while she contacted Mr Cohen on his extension.

'Mr Stern is here, sir,' she said.

She put the phone down.

'You can go in,' she indicated.

'Thank you.'

Jon went directly into Mr Cohen's office without knocking.

'Good morning,' he said.

Mr Cohen leaned back in his chair expansively.

'So!' he exclaimed.

Jon sat down in the chair opposite the desk.

'So!' Mr Cohen repeated.

Then he leaned forward in a business-like manner.

'You've certainly made a name for yourself, Jon. In more ways than one.'

'I'm afraid so,' admitted Jon.

'I didn't think much of your idea of a photo-call, if you remember.'

'No. You didn't.'

'But it seems to have worked. I've had dozens of calls from all over the world asking for you.'

'Vienna?'

'Nothing from Vienna.'

'I'm not surprised,' conceded Jon, glumly. 'Pity.'

'America appears to be particularly sympathetic, even amused.'

'Oh?'

'How does an American tour with your wife appeal to you?'

'Bartok?'

'Of course.'

'I can't believe it.'

'Jon, if you fell in a sewer you'd come out smelling of violets. You must have a guardian angel watching over you.'

'Must have,' admitted Jon, thinking of Jenni.

'The Americans appear to be as intrigued as much by your romantic antics as your playing.'

'I wish Vienna felt the same way. That's the one that worries me. I let them down. I said I'd do a concert free.'

'What is ten per cent of nothing?'

'I must compensate them in some way if we're back in business.'

'They may ask you back after the American tour.'

'Well, I'll tell Pam we're off again.'

He stood up and shook hands with Mr Cohen.

'Oh, by the way,' said Jon, 'could you arrange for the page turners to be boys this time?'

Mr Cohen chuckled. 'I'll see to it.'

'Good.'

Once outside the building, Jon stood on the pavement for a moment. He looked up at the sky and said, 'Thank you, Jenni.'

He then hurried home to Pam, who had been

worrying about the outcome of the interview. As soon as the front door opened she rushed to meet him.

'Well?' she asked, breathlessly.

'We're off to America,' said Jon.

'No!'

'Yes!'

Pam threw her arms round Jon's neck and he swung her round in a circle in the hall.

'What happened?' asked Pam, as they made their way to the sitting room.

'Well,' Jon began, ponderously. 'Evidently the Americans were intrigued by the photo-call and the little bust-up and get-together. It appealed to the romance in them.'

'Oh, I'm so relieved,' cried Pam.

'Incidentally, I asked for male page turners.'

'That's right. Be on the safe side.'

'It'll be your turn, dear.'

'I must tell Mother.'

'So must I.'

The newspapers were not slow to headline the story of the American tour, which, in turn, was picked up by the promoters in Vienna, who contacted Mr Cohen, who contacted Jon.

'I've had a feeler from Vienna,' he said.

'Oh, good,' enthused Jon.

'Nothing definite,' warned Mr Cohen. 'It all depends on the American tour. If that's a success I've an idea you'll be invited back.'

'Fingers crossed,' suggested Jon.

'Not on the piano, please,' entreated Mr Cohen.

'Oh, no!'

Jon put the phone down and turned to Pam.

'Did you hear that?'

'Of course not.'

'Mr Cohen's had a nibble from Vienna following the American deal.'

'Oh, good.'

'I'd like to make amends there.'

'I know you would.'

'You'd go again, wouldn't you? With the duets?'

'Of course.'

'I wonder if we could give them the *Radetzky March* as an encore? Really belt it out for them. Plenty of throbbing bass.'

'You'd better do the throbbing. My arms are not strong enough.'

'Shall we try it?'

'On one piano?'

'Yes. It'll give us an idea.'

Pam and Jon sat at the piano and started to play the Strauss march which they knew the Viennese loved so much. Half-way through Jon stopped.

'Don't you think the trio should be in octaves?' he suggested.

'Oh, no,' countered Pam. 'In unison if you like. Octaves take the heart out of it. Makes it too opaque.'

'Perhaps you're right.'

'In any case,' Pam reminded him, 'we don't know that we're going to Vienna yet.'

'No. We don't. What are we doing?'

They both laughed at the idea.

It was Jon's habit, before a tour, to visit his parents at their semi-detached house. He had not seen them since the unfortunate publicity and the Vienna debacle. They had spoken on the telephone and he had listened to all his mother's worries and anxieties about his future but now that all was forgiven if not forgotten by the media, both his mother and his father had accepted the phenomenon as something that happens to famous people. Because of the recent disruption between them, Jon wanted Pam to accompany him to the house. Pam was not all that keen on the idea in spite of the fact that, apart from being married to Jon, she was related to Mary and Sam. She thought that Jon should be left alone with his mother and father.

In the circumstances she was quite right. She couldn't help feeling out of place even as Mary threw her arms round Jon's neck and burst into tears. Sam gave him a hug and a pat on the back and all that Pam could do was watch.

'How long will you be away?' asked Mary.

'Several months,' said Jon.

'Months?' cried Mary, aghast. 'As long as that?'

'America's a big place, Mother.'

'You weren't so long last time,' Mary insisted.

'This is a more extensive tour,' Jon explained. 'More money, too,' he added for Sam's benefit.

'You'll look after him, won't you, Pam?' asked Mary.

'Of course.'

It was the only contribution she made to the conversation.

'Mr Cohen thinks we'll be invited back to Vienna,' said Jon.

'Oh, good,' enthused Mary.

'Does that mean another European tour?' asked Sam.

'No,' Jon replied. 'Only Vienna. I'm anxious to get my medals back there.'

'So I should think,' asserted Sam.

'Well,' said Jon, turning to Pam, 'we must be going.'

'You never stay long these days,' complained Mary.

'We'll come and see you again as soon as we get back,' promised Jon. 'Anything you want from the States, Dad?' he asked.

'No, thank you, son.'

'What about you, Mother?'

'Just you, dear.'

Mary was always tearful when she said goodbye to her son. Pleased as she was with his fantastic success, she still missed him when he was not at home in his room upstairs. She stayed at the gate and stood waving until Jon's car was out of sight. Even then she lingered before returning to the house and Sam with his television. When she shut the front door she could not help feeling that she was shutting something out. She didn't know what.

When she joined Sam in the sitting room she said, 'I always miss him when he goes abroad.'

'You shouldn't,' muttered Sam. 'He doesn't belong here any more.'

'Oh, I wouldn't say that.'

'His world is not ours.'

'How can you say that when he comes to see us before he goes away and when he comes back?'

'He doesn't stay long, you notice,' concluded Sam, grudgingly.

Mary did not pursue the conversation.

She could not understand her husband's attitude. At one time he was so excited and proud of Jon's achievement that he could not stop talking about it. He was embarrassed by the bad press the boy received when he got drunk in Vienna but that was all forgotten now. As a non-smoker and non-drinker he no doubt had principles of his own. She was aware that his colleagues at the office harassed him whenever Jon's name appeared in the papers, and that upset him. She even wondered if he wasn't a little jealous of his son, remembering that he was never keen on the boy's chosen career in the first place. He had wanted his son to be an accountant like himself. But no matter what her husband thought, she was happy and proud of her son.

The reception accorded Jon and Pam when they arrived in New York was nothing short of overwhelming. It seemed that they were welcomed as much as a romantic couple as acclaimed duettists. One or two of the newsmen made amusing reference to the fact that on this tour the page turners would be male.

The tour itself was a remarkable success, all the more remarkable since Bartok was not exactly a well-known or popular composer. Wherever Jon and Pam went they were feted. They were swamped with invitations and the media coverage was extensive, what with television and radio. By the time it came to return to London they were physically and mentally exhausted and for that reason chose to cross the Atlantic by ship so that they could rest.

They arrived home laden with presents for relatives and friends. Their first visit was to Pam's mother, who was still happily ensconced in her small hotel. On the same evening they drove down to Jon's home with gifts for Mary and Sam. Sam was so delighted at seeing them that Mary would not have thought that it was the same man who had moaned about living in different worlds. She didn't think it had anything to do with the presents that Jon had brought with him. For the first time, as if to confound him, the visitors stayed late. So late, in fact, that Mary, much to her delight, was able to give them a meal. Just like old times, she thought happily.

As hoped, following the obvious success of the

American tour, Mr Cohen was approached by the Vienna management with a view to a performance of the Bartok duets. He passed the invitation on to Jon, who did not need to be asked twice. He jumped at the chance. He couldn't wait to tell Pam or his mother, both of whom were delighted. Jon and Pam now set about refining their version of the *Radetzky March*, which they were playing when Pam asked, 'Are you sure this is a good idea?'

'Positive,' said Jon.

'It seems more like a vaudeville act.'

'Just you wait and see.'

'You're the boss,' concluded Pam.

In Vienna they again stayed at the Hotel Sacher and again Pam went shopping in the afternoon, but this time when she got back she found Jon on the bed alone. So she joined him.

At the concert Jon and Pam appeared on the stage together, hand in hand, to enthusiastic applause. They took their places at each piano and when the page turners came on there was a ripple of laughter as the audience noticed that they were both male students.

As soon as Jon and Pam began to play, the atmosphere was electric. They played superbly, better than they'd ever played before, and the audience rose to them. At the end of the programme, of course, there were calls for encores. It was known that Jon's finale was always the Liszt *Consolation*, and after that, nothing. On this occasion, however, as Jon and Pam stood at their pianos they looked across at each other and smiled. Jon nodded to Pam and they took to their seats again. They waited, allowing the audience to enjoy the anticipation. Then, as the first recognisable notes of the *Radetzky*

March were heard, there was laughter and applause, the audience beating out the rhythm with their hands as was their ritual.

Jon and Pam threw themselves happily into the famous march and at the end of it there was a crash of applause and stamping of feet and loud cries of 'Bravo'. The noise was deafening. Jon and Pam got up from their seats. Jon bowed, Pam curtsied and then they were gone from the stage, never to appear again. Except, perhaps, at some future date.

The newspapers next morning were unanimous. 'ALL IS FORGIVEN' screamed the headlines, ending with the most congratulatory eulogy that any artistes could wish for.

Before they left for home, of course, the two duettists were invited to parties all over Vienna. Needless to say, newsmen and cameramen covered the departure.

As Jon and Pam sat together in the plane, Jon said, 'Any concert after that will be an anti-climax.'

'I wonder,' mused Pam.

'Why?' asked Jon, slightly puzzled.

'I'm pregnant.'

'What!' shouted Jon, in alarm.

'Ssh!' warned Pam.

'Should you be flying?' asked Jon anxiously.

'Well, I can't get out and run.'

'Don't worry. We'll see a doctor as soon as we reach home.'

'It's early days yet. It may even be a false alarm.'

'Don't say that.'

'You're pleased, are you?'

'Pleased? I'm delighted. I'm head over heels. Aren't you?'

'Of course.'

The media reception committee in England were full of questions about the reception in Vienna. They had read the news of the triumph but wanted more details, and Jon told them all they wanted to know.

'Incidentally, you can congratulate my wife on turning a duet into a trio,' he added.

'Jon! No!' cried Pam.

'I leave you to work it out,' said Jon, as he and Pam made their way to the car.

'You shouldn't have said that,' admonished Pam.

'Why not? I want everyone to know.'

'You'll look a fool if it's a false alarm.'

'Darling, when we get home we'll make sure it's not a false alarm.'

'Here we go again,' chuckled Pam, *sotto voce.*

Newspaper stories of Pam's pregnancy caused Sam Stern, in his usual grudging tone, to complain.

'You see? They tell the world before they tell us. We're only the grandparents.'

'Oh, I don't suppose it was like that. I expect they could see she was pregnant.'

'Didn't look like it when she was here, when they came with their presents. Flat as a board. They could have told us then.'

'They didn't even tell Louise.'

'What's the point? Tell the press not us?'

'They probably wanted to tell the first person they met, in their excitement. I'm very pleased for them, aren't you?'

'Oh, yes. Come to that, yes.'

'After all, they're public figures now.'

'If it's a boy I suggest they call it Samuel.'

'You would. What if it's a girl?'

'Then Samantha.'

'You're determined to get in, aren't you.'

They both laughed.

Both mothers fussed over Pam during her pregnancy. Hardly a day went by without one or the other telephoning with questions and advice as if they were the only women to have given birth. Both Jon and Pam bore the well-meaning attentions with equanimity. They spent the pregnancy in Monte Carlo but moved later to their house in Avenue Road, North London, where they felt they'd get better medical attention.

The baby was born in the London Clinic. It was a girl, which both Pam and Jon had hoped for. Very soon they were all back together. A nanny was installed in the house and Pam could look forward to nursing her daughter in the garden.

'Not too much sun, remember,' warned Jon as they sat there one morning.

As the sun went behind the clouds Pam said, 'It's not all that warm here. I'm taking her in.'

Jon stayed in the garden while Pam carried the baby indoors. He was alone and felt at peace.

'This is where I really do leave you, Jon,' said Jenni.

Jon turned suddenly, not knowing where to look.

'Jenni!' he cried, delightedly but quietly.

'You have a lovely little girl to look after now and she will inspire you in your work. You will take her and Pam on your tours and there's no reason why you shouldn't be very happy.'

'I'm sure we will. But why do you have to go, Jenni?'

'It's time.'

'Oh, no. Don't go. Please.'

'I must.'

'But why? You went away before and came back. Can't you do it again?'

'No. I'm afraid not. I came to help you and I've done that. You don't need my help now.'

'I do, Jenni. I do. I'll be lost without you.'

'No, you won't. You may think you will but you won't.'

'You make it sound so final.'

'It is. You must face it, Jon.'

'I'll never forget you, Jenni.'

'Thank you.'

'I'll always think you're near.'

'I will be.'

'Oh, Jenni. Don't go.'

'I must. I'll be watching you. I'll know what you're doing. You can talk to me. I'll hear you, but I can't talk to you any more.'

'That's what I'll miss.'

'It won't be necessary. You'll see.'

'Oh, Jenni. I'll miss you so much.'

'Goodbye, Jon.'

'Jenni!'

Tears filled his eyes as he looked into space, searching for his friend. He turned this way and that, as if lost, which he was.

'Jenni,' he whispered. 'Jenni…'

He stood in the garden, wanting to stay in the same place in case Jenni should come back, but he knew in his heart that she wouldn't. Slowly he left the garden, still looking up into the sky, and went indoors reluctantly. When Pam saw him she was puzzled by his appearance.

'You alright?' she asked. 'You look as if you've been crying.'

'There's a bit of a breeze out there,' Jon explained.

To cover his confusion he went over to his daughter as she nestled in Pam's arms, and stroked her soft cheek. He hugged them both.

'Bless you, sweethearts.'

Later that day Pam produced a piece of paper with a list of names on it.

'I've made a list of names for the christening,' she said. 'See what you think.'

Jon studied the paper, then he put it aside.

'Do you know what I'd like to call her?'

'What?'

'Jenni. With an "i"!'

'Jenni? Where did you get that name from?'

'It just came to me.'

'Jenni,' mused Pam. 'I like that. Jenni it is.'

'Jenni…' breathed Jon.